MARK ANCHOVY

PIZZA POWER

D1100856

C3   2009

MARK ANCHOVY

PIZZA POWER

William Goldsmith

Piccadilly
PRESS

First published in Great Britain in 2022 by
PICCADILLY PRESS
Bonnier Books UK
4th Floor, Victoria House
Bloomsbury Square
London WC1B 4DA
Owned by Bonnier Books
Sveavägen 56, Stockholm, Sweden

Text and illustrations © William Goldsmith 2022

All rights reserved.
No part of this publication may be reproduced, stored or transmitted
in any form or by any means, electronic, mechanical, photocopying or
otherwise, without the prior written permission of the publisher.

The right of William Goldsmith to be identified as the author and
illustrator of this work has been asserted by him in accordance with
the Copyright, Designs and Patents Act 1988.

This is a work of fiction. Names, places, events and incidents are either
the products of the author's imagination or used fictitiously.
Any resemblance to actual persons, living or dead, is purely coincidental.

A CIP catalogue record for this book is available from the British Library.

ISBN: 978-1-80078-042-2
Also available as an ebook and audiobook

1
Printed and bound in Great Britain by Clays Ltd, Elcograf S.p.A.

Piccadilly Press is an imprint of Bonnier Books UK
www.bonnierbooks.co.uk

To Koroku

Chapter 1

hen I got fired from the G.S.L.,
Princess Skewer told me that great
power brought great responsibility.
I'd been given an apprentice detective to train, so
I already knew that. I just didn't expect harpoon
guns, ransom and quite so many fish guts. Or that
my apprentice would be my sister. The trouble
began before we'd even left Rufflington-on-Sea.
We were in my secret office (which still didn't have
a hot tub) when the pizza phone rang.

RINNGGGGGGGG!

My sister upended a milkshake on my desk.

'Alicia, that's gone all over my brief!' I shouted. 'Woah, what are you doing?!!'

RINNGGGGGGGG!

'Just mopping it up with these scraps of paper, Colin, chillax . . .'

'Those are the pages of an important report! Get a cloth! And call me "Anchovy" at work!'

RINNGGGGGGGG!

'When do I get a G.S.L. codename then?'

'Soon. Hello?'

'_Hi there, little buddy,_' a gruff voice snorted. '_Did you miss us?_'

I groped for my swivel chair. I would have sat down were it not for the Fruit Pastilles, comic and toy donkey that _someone_ had strewn over it.

'_You still there, little buddy?_'

They'd found me. Finally. And they'd come back to finish the job. A snippier voice now joined the line.

'Where is that disgusting little boy? Give me the phone, Brutus! Heidi is very, very cross!'

The henchman I dodged in Rome? The jewel-thief I followed to Moscow? Together? When? Where? How?!!

'Col– I mean, *Anchovy* – are you okay?' whispered Alicia. 'Your face looks like a vom-job.'

'Listen here, young man!' barked Heidi. 'You'd better watch your stepffffffffffffffff . . .'

The voice dissolved into the static of laughter.

'Yelena!' I shouted. 'Yaconda! That is *not* funny!'

Alicia frowned beneath her wonky fringe. She still hadn't met Yelena and Yaconda, the famous impressionist twins from the Golden Spatula League. They were forever slipping into different voices, trying them on for size.

'Sorry, Anchovy,' said Yelena, now in a cooing pigeon voice. 'Just head up to the shop floor. The call for a Mark Anchovy pizza will come in a minute.'

'With extra anchovies,' said Yaconda, speaking like a Victorian-cockney policeman. 'You know the drill.'

'Okay.'

'You've read the brief, right, Anch?'

I glanced at the pages in the puddle of milkshake.

'Mostly.'

'See ya later, little buddy!!' they said, switching back to henchman voice, then they hung up.

I slung on my trench coat – well, my mum's trench coat – and loaded up my molten-tomato-purée gun.

'Alicia,' I said. 'This is a warm-up for your first practical test as an apprentice for the Golden Spatula League. It's very important that you do what I say, when I say it.'

I went over to the dented can of chopped tomatoes that activated the fake door. 'First, go up to our room and switch on the recording of you practising the double bass. Then take the back door, put on your helmet and find my bike. There's a new, extra-large satchel box on it.' I spoke slowly so my apprentice could understand. 'Do you know the one I mean?'

'Yeah . . . what do you want me to do?'

I twiddled the dented can.

'Get in it.'

'Er, what?! Into the pizza satchel? I'm a detective, aren't I? Since when do detectives –'

'You're an apprentice. And you've got five minutes.'

Her blonde fringe billowed as she huffed.

'Don't worry, Al. There'll be breathing holes and it's only until we're off Brayne Road. Okay?'

She nodded.

'Okay, let's go.'

She scuttled up to our room while I went into

our parents' Ancient-Rome-themed pizzeria.
They'd snazzed it up recently, thanks to a donation
from a mystery customer. By which I mean my
G.S.L. salary. They'd kept the plastic grapevine,
though, and the statue of Markus Anchovius, and
the fridge that droned at an insanely loud volume.
Speaking of insanely loud volume, my mum was on
the phone. My dad was scattering flour.

'Yes-yes, yes-yes!' said my mum, in her super-
polite phone voice. 'Colin will come right away,
yes-yes!! What did you say your name was? Oh, it's
French? Yes-yes, how interesting. Well, goodbye,
Miss, er . . . *Bobo*.'

'Funny,' said my dad, his monobrow rising,
'how more and more people seem to be ordering
"extra anchovies". A year ago, it was unheard of.'

The *dum-de-dum-dum* of Alicia's bass playing
'Hot Cross Buns' broke the tension. It was a clever
G.S.L. recording with pauses, mistakes and the odd

yowl of frustration. My dad whirled the dough. My mum passed me the order and turned down my collar. Well, her collar. I turned it back up.

The recording switched to the bassline for James Bond. It's three notes. And, when you're trying to focus on a case, could be a slow-burn form of torture. The cheesy, salty-fishy waft of a cooked Mark Anchovy pizza zephyred across the counter. My dad boxed it up and I took it out to my bike. I guessed Alicia was in place.

'Hang in there, Al,' I whispered to the satchel box.

'HURRY UP,' replied the breathing hole. I slid the pizza in with Alicia and zipped up the top.

'Don't go too fast!' cooed my mum. *I couldn't if I wanted to*, I thought, as I strained every calf sinew to pedal off.

It was a typical spring evening in Rufflington – a tinge of sun, but with clouds rolling in like fat caterpillars. There were lawn mowers spewing grass, scabby teens sharing candy floss, seagulls circling and a metal detectorist pottering on the beach.

'You can open the lid now,' I called as I heaved us under the railway arches. Alicia poked her head out.

'So, I've been thinking about my codename,' she shouted as we sped over the Eight Dials Crossroads.

'Sure . . .'

'Shall I read the list?'

'How big is it?'

'Option One: Alcatraz.'

'That's a prison.'

'Option Two: Oi Oi Saveloy?'

'Not really a name.'

'Julia Seize Ya?'

'Please, no. How about . . . Sister Salad?'

'That makes me sound like a nun!'

'Let's come back to this, all right?'

A salty blast barrelled onto the seafront as we headed to our destination: the old slot-machine parlour. No one used it these days, so the human weasel at the till did a double take when we entered. He switched off the shoebox-sized TV and put on yellow-tinged glasses.

'There was a pizza order,' I said. 'From Caesar Pizza?'

The weasel nodded to the back, towards a riot of zaps, pops and *neeeowwwww* sounds.

'What. A. Creepazoid,' said Alicia, at her usual volume.

We rounded a bank of ancient arcade machines. Someone shrieked: 'Come on! Come on! Die, die, die, die!!'

Hunched in a monster-truck-shaped machine, bounding over moonlit craters and zapping alien armies, was a teenage girl in an olive-green blazer,

white breeches and shiny black boots. A horse-
jockey helmet lay on the floor.

'Aarrrgh!' she wailed, as 'GAME OVER' letters
dissolved on the screen. She flicked a mini-plait
from her amber-coloured eyes and thumped the
controls. Alicia flinched. I re-read my mum's note.

'Are you . . . Isadora Bobo?'

'Are you Detective Mark Anchovy?' she tilted her head. 'I was expecting someone older.'

'My apprentice and I have brought your pizza, with extra anchovies,' I said, grabbing the box from Alicia. I was shocked by how light it was. She didn't even blink.

'You do realise,' I muttered through gritted teeth, 'that these pizzas are an important alibi.'

'Alibi . . .' mumbled Alicia. 'Maybe my codename could be Allie Alibi?'

'Oh, what a shame,' said Isadora Bobo, surveying the remaining slice and a half. 'I really *love* anchovies. But Mummy doesn't allow them.'

'Most people hate them,' I said, glaring at Alicia. I took out my mentor's logbook and turned to a table entitled 'Catalogue of Apprentice Misdemeanours and Offences'. Next to today's date I added: 'Ate an important alibi.'

'It doesn't really matter, I suppose,' said Isadora,

gesturing for us to sit at the controls of a mocked-up spaceship. 'We both know that we're not really here to talk about pizza.' She reached into her jacket and pulled out a plastic folder, decorated with the badges of a football team I really can't stand. She unbuttoned the folder and brought out a light-blue, spatula-embossed calling card.

'I picked up your card, Detective Anchovy, while using the bathroom of an insalubrious restaurant in Central London. I think it was called Fryer Tuck's.'

'What does "insta-loo-brush" mean?' said Alicia.

'Gross, I think,' I said. 'She's talking about the G.S.L. Headquarters.'

'Yes. It *was* gross. But I suppose,' continued Isadora, 'that not many people go into a greasy-spoon diner if they want an elite detective agency. So I imagine you only deal with very special cases.'

She left her pizza crust, which my mum would have hated. 'And I promise you that what I have to relate is a very special case.'

'What can we do for you, Miss Bobo?'

'Find my father.' Isadora reached into her football folder. 'Lord Bobo.'

'*Lord Bobo?*' asked Alicia.

'He's been missing for some time,' sighed Isadora. 'There have been sightings of him in the past year. He was apparently spotted in Venezuela. In Goa. In the Faroe Islands. All false leads.' She passed us a clipping from an old TV guide. 'This is soooo embarrassing,' said Isadora. 'But he was a gameshow host in the 90s. It was super-popular until it got axed in 2000. Here's his photo.'

It showed a beaming, bowler-hatted man, complete with moustache and monocle.

'I was told that if anyone could find him,' Isadora stood up, 'it would be the Golden Spatula

League. Plus . . . yours was the nicest-looking face in the directory.'

'Haaaaaaaaaa!' blurted Alicia as I visibly melted.

Isadora collected her helmet. 'I must get back to the riding school or Mummy will be furious! But please, anything you can do to find him. Anything.'

We followed her out onto the seafront, where she waved to a sage-green, chauffeur-driven car.

'I worry,' said Isadora, as her driver opened the door, 'that someone wants him dead.'

'Ooooooft,' said Alicia.

'Try not to worry,' I said, even though she had sent me smack bang into worry-town.

Isadora Bobo gave a grim half-smile and sped off.

Chapter 2

I knew the headteacher's office like the back of my hand. Behind the frosted glass, the Michelin-man silhouette of my history teacher, Mr Hogstein, protested my guilt to Mrs Z.

'I've had it!' he bellowed. 'I've had it with this boy, Pauline! The scandal in Rome! The assault in Moscow! He's a maniac, I tell you, a maniac!'

'Arnold, will you please lower your voice?'

'Why, the school play last term . . . I was almost *assassinated*, Pauline! And now this!'

Quiet mode for Hogstein was still pretty shouty.

'I recognise that today has been extremely distressing for you, Arnold, but –'

'Pauline! Don't tell me the board of governors intends to let this renegade off the hook *again*?!'

'Arnold – I appreciate your agitation, but this boy has been vouched for by a high-ranking governmental body whose details I cannot reveal. I confess I am unfamiliar with this logo of cooking spatulas – or is it rowing oars? – but our legal department has assured us that the letter is genuine. We have no choice but to allow Colin Kingsley to continue his studies at Rufflington Community School.'

There was a hoggish gasp as a ham-fist thumped a desk.

'What utter ROT! I've had it. I've had it! I resign! This school is rotten! Rotten to the core!'

'Arnold. Are you being serious?'

'I've never been so serious in all my life! I will

never darken the doorways of this madhouse again! I'm leaving! Hell, I might even leave the country once and for all! I want to be as far as humanly possibly from that TERROR, Colin Kingsley!'

'Well, in that case, we wish you well in your next venture, Arnold. You've certainly been a, um, *unique* teacher.'

The door crashed open and my nemesis charged out. He saw me, turned every shade of purple and stomped off. I was summoned into Mrs Z's office.

'Hello, Colin,' she said. 'Can you please explain what happened today?'

Could I? In every sense of the word, it had been a total washout . . .

No one was interested in this Duke of Basingstoke hiking award. Especially not with Hogstein at the helm. Even on the minibus the omens looked bad. If I can call it a minibus – it was more like a bucking bronco as it bounced along the forest tracks. You either banged your head or felt your stomach do backflips. I gripped my absurdly heavy rucksack and prayed it would end. Robin was drooling in his sleep. And he was dangerously close to using my shoulder as a pillow. Dexter, the playground despot, sat behind with his cronies. They were poised with marker pens. Hogstein – as usual – was oblivious. He kept his Hog-stare on me. Some of my G.S.L. missions had sort of interfered with school life, and I guess he did take a slight dusting. And because of some fire-related incidents, he had told the school counsellor I was a 'pie-maniac'. Which was rich.

He cleared his throat. 'Ahem . . . boys and girls, may I have your attention, please? Orienteering is a wonderful skill. I have every confidence that our camping trip in the Forest of Pottingbean will be a magical experience for everyone. The stillness of being one with nature. Living off the land, like the ancient hunter-gatherers of prehistoric Britain.'

Anabel blew bubblegum. Laetitia rolled her eyes.
I heard marker lids squeak off their pens.

'Just imagine, a time when children *your* age
would already be building their own wattle-and-
daub shelter! Weaving their own baskets! Spearing
their own wild boar! Foraging for roots and berries!
Gathering their nuts for the winter!'

'Gathering their *what*, sir?!' bawled Dexter the
human dung beetle.

'For goodness' sake, Dexter will you gr– Wait,
who's drawn that curly moustache on Robin's face?
Come on! Who was it?! Wake him up, Colin!'

The latest crater shook our moon buggy so
much that I didn't have to.

'Wuh?' Robin croaked.

'I need to be sick, sir!' wailed Maisie.

'Me too!' said Dania.

'Me three!' said Adam.

The minibus stopped.

'OPEN THE DOOORS!!!!!!' pleaded Miss
Odedra.

'Mayday, mayday, mayday!' shouted Dexter, in
idiot-heaven.

We jumped out just as the rain began lashing
down with a fury Hogstein would've been proud
of. So as well as having to mop up a sea of puke,
we also looked like a bag of drowned rats. Once
the teachers had split us into groups and our pots,
pans, maps, camping stoves, compasses, first-aid
kits and everything but the kitchen sink had been
distributed, we set forth into the forest to get all
prehistoric. Anabel and Laetitia craned over a map.
Hogstein tried to stop Dexter from lobbing rocks
at a squirrel. I told Robin I was going off for a pee
and that I'd catch them up. When they were out
of sight, I lugged the small house off my back and
opened the top flap. A head wriggled out.

'You okay, Al?'

'Your chocolate bars helped.'

'Bars? Plural?'

'I left half a Bounty. Not my fave, to be honest.'

'Get out and put your mac on.'

'Sheesh!' She looked dismayed at our soggy surroundings. 'Is this what big school's like?'

I tried to cheer her up.

'Good job staying so hidden! I don't think anyone heard you in there.'

I opened the mentor's logbook and put an emphatic tick next to 'Elementary Contortion, Practical Exam: Exercise One – Rucksacks and/or Suitcases.' It was handy that she was fairly mini for her age.

'Okay, Exercise Two,' I continued. 'What do we do if we need to get away from some teachers? For G.S.L. purposes only, of course.'

Alicia concentrated.

'Phone those weirdo twins and get them to do an impression of one teacher telling the other teacher they've got you and not to worry?'

'You learn fast, sis.' I flipped open the pizza watch and dialled the twins.

'When will I get one of those watches?'

'Soon. Yaconda, Yelena?'

'Hi, Anch. How's the hike?'

'Wet. Phase One of my apprentice's exam is underway. Proceed with the Hog-con.'

'Got it,' said Yelena.

'Who's the other teacher you're with?' said Yaconda.

'Miss Odedra.'

'Oh yeah, that's an easy one,' they said in Miss Odedra's voice.

'Oh, while I've got you,' I said, 'any leads on the Bobo case I sent in yesterday?'

'Yeah, Princess Skewer told us you were on that

job, Anch,' said Yelena. 'I sounded the alarm across the different branches.'

'Actually, Lena,' said Yaconda, '*I* sounded the alarm to the different branches.'

'Whatever, Yack . . . Anyway, Anchovy, yeah, we're looking into it.'

'Thanks,' I said. 'I guess I'd better get back to mentoring.'

Taking out my G.S.L. map, we scrambled up a muddy bank to a winding path strewn with pinecones. We clambered over the roots of ancient trees, whose branches looped through the forest like the tentacles of a giant, mossy octopus.

'Exercise Three,' I continued, starting to feel – shudder – a bit like Hogstein. 'And this is a twenty-pointer. It's called –'

'The Secret Bunker Test. Yeah, I read the paper, Col.'

'Call me Anchovy! You'll need this.' I passed her

a special flashlight. 'Camillo, our G.S.L. inventor, made it. It's a kind of infrared/high-vis/X-ray torch.'

'Haaaa, you're wearing Y-fronts! Run out of boxers?'

'Point that away from me. It's for detecting unexpected materials that have been camouflaged to look like something else.'

'So I'm looking for some weird metal levers or hinges or keyholes that are hidden in a bush or something?'

She seemed to enjoy zipping it around as we ambled over rocks and fallen trees, hugging the river that sloshed alongside us. The rain died down. We came to a clearing with a waterfall cascading below. Shards of rainbow arced in its froth.

'This is actually quite fun, Col – I mean, Anchovy,' said Alicia. 'Woah, I think the torch is doing something!' A bulb glowed green as she shone it on the base of an exceptionally big tree.

'What are you thinking, Al?'

'I'm thinking my codename could be Sergeant Pepperoni?'

'About the tree.'

'Oh.' She gave it a kick. 'Seems pretty hollow.'

'Don't bash it! What if there's a criminal hiding in there?'

'Cool! Is there?'

I shrugged. 'Think about our secret office. How do you get in?'

'Oh yeah . . . the dented tomato can that you twist.' Her eyes darted around. She began twisting rocks and twigs until she got it. A very convincing mushroom.

'Gently, don't break it.'

She twisted the mushroom. There was an instant juddering, like a ramp going down on a freight ship, as the tree began to move. Thankfully the waterfall partly drowned out the noise. Bits of moss fell off the trunk until we saw a set of hinges.

'Stand–back–stand–back–stand–back,' megaphoned a robot voice, and the fake tree gradually tilted, landing on the opposite riverbank. The remaining stump now revealed a hole with ladder rungs inside. We lowered ourselves in.

'Wooooooooah,' said Alicia. It was a proper survival bunker – with a bed, blankets, food, a heater and Trivial Pursuit. I'd seen something similar in Italy.

'Good place to come if there's a zombie apocalypse,' I said. 'Okay, Exercise Four. If you get this, you'll have an excellent chance of going on the assignment next week.'

'Next week! So you're not *really* spending half-term with Robin's family in Cornwall?'

'No.'

'What will *I* tell M and D, though?'

'The G.S.L. can arrange a band camp or
something. They mentioned the National
Children's Jazz Orchestra. But let's not get ahead of
ourselves. First you need to –'

I was going to say 'scan for fingerprints' when
something outside bellowed. I stuck my head out of
the stump. Although it sounded exactly like an orc
with anger-management issues whose mother you'd
accidentally insulted, it wasn't. Striding across the
river via the fallen fake tree in a fluorescent orange
poncho, his glasses misted up, was the President
of the Anti-Colin Club, Mr Hogstein. A stunned
group of kids watched from the opposite bank.

'I KNEW IT!' Hogstein bellowed. 'That trail of
chocolate-bar wrappers gave you away, Kingsley!!
I *knew* something was fishy! HOW DARE YOU
RUN AWAY FROM YOUR GROUP! HOW
DARE YOU!'

Alicia poked her head out of the stump, jostling

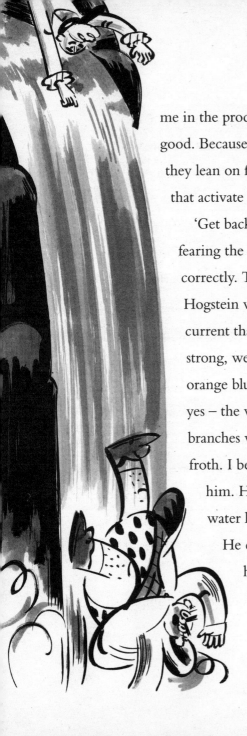

me in the process. Jostling is never good. Because when people jostle, they lean on fake mushroom levers that activate fake trees.

'Get back, sir!!!' I shouted, fearing the worst. I feared correctly. The tree went up. Mr Hogstein went down. As the current that carried him was so strong, we just saw a fluorescent orange blur haring towards — yes — the waterfall. Some scraggly branches were sticking into the froth. I begged them to catch him. He surfaced, spewing water like a Roman fountain. He clawed at a branch, but his hood fell over his eyes. He buffeted on.

His glasses were long gone.

Considering she'd just pressed the red button for all-out nuclear warfare, Alicia's response was impressive. She sprinted over the rocks to the waterfall's edge, feeding a new branch towards Hogstein. He bounced towards her, dodgems-esque. The branch caught him, snagging in his belt hole. But the current was too strong. It sucked him away from his belt – and, unfortunately, his trousers. These now shredded off like a never-ending handkerchief from a conjurer's sleeve. Over he went. In the rumbles of the waterfall, we could just about catch the reverberating cries: 'YOU'LL PAY FOR THIS, KINGSLEEEEYYYY YYYYYYYYYYYYYYYYYYYYYyyyyy!'

There was probably a good – what? – twenty feet of waterfall. It was a horrible moment. We peered into the abyss. After what felt like an age, the fluorescent poncho bobbed to the surface, finally resting against a rockpool. For a while I was unsure if he was moving or if it was just the motions of the rapids. My throat dried up. The whole forest seemed silent. We waited. We watched. The other kids bowed their heads. I've never been so thankful to hear that nasal voice distantly splutter: 'You'll – *(choke)* – pay for this, Kingsley – *(choke)* – you'll – *(choke)* – pay for this!'

By some miracle he dragged himself onto the distant bank and lay on his back, resuming the Roman-fountain impression. Alicia looked up at me and pursed her lips.

'So . . . did I pass?'

Chapter 3

You don't pack much for a G.S.L assignment. A toothbrush, a purée gun, a change of trench coat. I imagined what scenery lay behind the grimy train window. There'd be a moon, a moor, a bridge, a dirt track leading to a crumbling mansion. My classmates were in Cornwall, or France, or Spain, wedging little shells onto elaborate sandcastles. Not me.

The guard announced the second-last stop, then tickled the pug belonging to the only other passenger. I went to the loo. As arranged, a tuxedo was hanging from the door hook. A briefcase was under the sink. A musical triangle was hidden in the towel dispenser. For realism, I flushed, and then donned the tux. The bow tie was tricky. A map and floorplan were in the top pocket, printed on edible paper. I would say it was chocolate mousse flavoured. The train creaked into Magnor Weevis.

With my photographic memory, and no wayward sisters to herd, the schlep along country lanes was fine. As advertised, there was the moon, the moor, the bridge, the mansion. Alicia was in there, double-bassing away. Amazing how an apprentice these days could land their first gig in what was basically Downton Abbey. I'd spent my first assignment squashed in a moving wheelie bin with my face in a sick bag. I guess it made sense. You have an orchestra of kids going hell for leather; you park them in a big house in the back of beyond.

As I approached the old pile using the gardener's

gate, I recognised the brassy parps flying from the French windows. Alicia had said it was the theme tune from *Peter Gum* or something. Plucking, glocking, trumpeting, woodwinding, drum-beating in the orange glow were rows of other children, also in tuxedoes. I could see Alicia's double bass. But no Alicia. Perfect.

Skirting along the ivy, I rapped on the kitchen door and chanted: *'Aureum in spatha est . . . vivat in spatha.'* I was let in by a girl with an expression that matched the salmon she was about to fillet. I thanked her, brought up my mental photograph and snaked around the appropriate wood-panelled, stuffed-bear-lined corridor. Whoever had bought this ancient manor had amassed a ton of bric-a-brac. One door was flanked by old diver suits, complete with harpoon guns and crusty sea chests.

I found the musicians' changing room. I glanced at the pizza watch, knocked and slid open the door.

The pounding brass riff from the hall gave the illusion that, for once, things were going smoothly. Of course, I should've known, two major assignments in, that the word 'smooth' doesn't exist in G.S.L-speak.

'May I help you, young man?' It was a polite, honeyed, kindly voice.

I turned to face what I presumed was a butler. I didn't actually think they existed in real life. He didn't have a silver platter, but apart from that he was fully butlered up. The tailcoat; the waistcoat; the black tie; winged collar; white gloves; grey, faintly pinstriped trousers and a starchy white cloth draped over the arm. He was balding and wore glasses that magnified his eyes ten-fold. I brought out the triangle and tinged it.

'I'm with the orchestra.'

'I see, sir. And may I ask why you aren't playing in the current number?'

'There isn't a triangle part. And I left my glasses in the changing room.'

'Then why, may I ask, did you knock?'

'Because . . . ah . . .' The brain pot-holed for a minute, then found an extra gear. 'Because, well, I didn't want to walk in on anyone in their birthday suit, if you know what I mean.'

'I see.'

He blinked, spun like a spring-powered robot and floated off. A **beep** on my pizza watch announced the words: **Assemble and head to the moor in five minutes – P.A.**

'P.A.'? Some typo by Princess Skewer?

What am I looking for out there? I typed.

Something pretty hard to miss, was the helpful reply.

I nipped into the changing room. The double-bass case was in the corner. I flipped it open.

'Sometime this millennium would be nice,' said

Alicia, snuggled inside like an Egyptian mummy.

'Sorry, Al,' I said, and threw her an overpriced packet of Fruit Pastilles from the train. 'I was delayed by the butler.'

'Butler?' She inhaled a lucky run of two red pastilles followed by two black ones. 'There's no butler here.'

There was a cough and a clicking outside.

'Okay, Al, I'm buckling up. Hold on.'

She squidged back into her musical sarcophagus and I slung the case onto my back. We left the changing room and I tried to remember the nearest exit in my brain map. I got it – a tall, pointy arch with a shield above it. There was just one problem. My old pal the butler was standing in it. With a harpoon gun.

'You now appear to play the double bass, Mr Anchovy,' he purred. 'How virtuosic of you.'

Spinning behind the nearest stuffed bear seemed a better option than trying to work out what 'virtuosic' meant. The resulting *THUD* confirmed this. I was sorry the bear had to cop it, though; he had a cuddly face. *THUD!* seconded the butler. How many harpoons does a harpoon gun hold?

'What's going on!!!' Alicia banged inside the case.

'All fine, don't worry,' I said, setting the heat on the purée gun to 'Turbo'. I fired between the bear's legs, once, twice, three times a butler, and legged it to the opposite corridor. From the hall, I could hear the brass section really hitting their stride. I jumped up a level. But this bit of corridor wasn't in my brain map – it ended in a stained-glass window. The tailcoated terror staggered around the corner. He harpooned again, now catching a banister.

I didn't think from this point on. I just lasered the window and leapt into the garden. So much for smoothness. I fired the last shreds of purée at the figure lumbering after me, the white gloves bobbing in the dark. He took a tumble. A rabbit hole? A bog? As I tore over the bridge, the bushes began to ripple violently, whipped up by a great gale. I now saw the unmissable landmark I was supposed to head to. An aeroplane, roaring on the moor.

Chapter 4

The cabin door opened and two identical figures, each with blue-and-pink dyed hair, fed out a ladder. Yaconda took the double-bass case. Yelena took my briefcase. They greeted me in the butler's voice. It wasn't appreciated. We released Alicia.

'Ooh, it's Anchovy's new apprentice!' the twins said in unison. 'What's your codename?'

'Maybe Tina Tuna?' said Alicia.

'We're still deciding,' I said.

The plane had five lounge chairs, spatula-patterned carpeting, a minibar, and a door marked

'Private'. By this sat an annoyingly handsome, golden-curled boy, glued to a laptop. He was wearing a red sweatband as well as a tank-top, presumably to show off his biceps. Or, as Dexter would call them, 'guns'. Alicia jumped in a chair and set it to recline mode. The plane gathered pace and off we whooshed, the manor below twinkling in the moonlit fields.

'The boss'll be out in a minute,' said Yelena in a husky thug voice. She went behind the minibar and poured Fanta and Ribena into a cocktail shaker. 'Yack, did you phone the orchestra conductor as these guys' parents saying that –'

'– Alicia had gone home? Yeah, I did that like twenty minutes ago, Lena!'

'All right, all right . . . Anyone want a Ribanta?'

Alicia took a sip and Roman-fountained it out, just as a whopping pair of trainers stepped out of

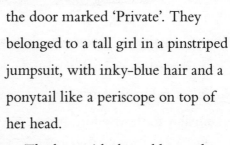

the door marked 'Private'. They belonged to a tall girl in a pinstriped jumpsuit, with inky-blue hair and a ponytail like a periscope on top of her head.

The boy with the golden curls leapt to attention and chirruped: 'Princess Skewer! I was just going to alert you . . .'

She made a flapping gesture and eyed me. Then she eyed the Ribanta streaming down Alicia's tuxedo.

'You're late, Anchovy.'

'The butler did it.'

'I'm sorry?'

'Never mind.'

'I won't. Step this way.'

The twins gave us a quadruple eyebrow raise as we followed Princess Skewer into her inner sanctum. The word 'plush' sprang to mind. I wondered how much the antique chess table cost. And the dispenser of star-shaped ice cubes. And how it was possible to have a mini aquarium on a plane. It can't have been fun for the seahorses.

Golden Boy hovered behind Princess, a moth to her flame. Princess swivelled in a chair and grabbed a projector clicker. 'Oh, have you met my PA, P.A.?'

Golden Boy beamed as if he'd only just noticed

the non-models in the room. 'Oh hiiiiiiiii, so nice to meet you guys! I'm Pierce Aniseed. I'll be your go-to guy if you have any questions for our wonderful leader, Princess Skewer. Can I get you a Ribanta, Princess?'

'Not now, thanks, Pierce. Yes?'

Alicia had raised her hand. 'Um, where are we going?'

'Japan.'

'Cooooooooooooooooool!!!!'

'Why Japan?' I asked.

'Because we've found Lord Bobo.'

'You've found Lord Bobo? Already?'

Pierce Aniseed snorted. Princess twisted her ponytail.

'For pitta's sake, Anchovy!' she said. 'Don't you read the G.S.L. bulletin? Lord Bobo was spotted in a ramen bar in Tokyo yesterday.

He's slightly changed in appearance, though. Pierce, if you will . . .'

'Right away, Princess!!' beamed Pierce Aniseed, and he rolled down a projection screen.

'This,' said Princess, clicking her clicker, 'was Lord Bobo in his hey-day.'

The screen swarmed with multicoloured stars, fizzing like atoms, over a fake castle, lemon yellow with ramparts and turrets, a drawbridge and moat. It sparkled as if lathered in sequin-filled shower gel. A trancey synthesiser pumped a beat. A studio audience whooped and cheered. The camera panned over the drawbridge and through a set of candy-striped doors. A drum roll struck up. Harps began lullabying. A smooth, bassy voice announced: 'And here is your host . . . LORD BO-BOOOOOOOOOOOOOOOOOOOOOOOOO!!'

Isadora's father was a lanky man in pink-and-green tweed, a gold-and-navy-striped waistcoat,

 high-vis green shirt, purple bow tie, yellow socks, red bowler hat and a monocle. An immaculate white moustache and mega-watt smile gleamed amid this human rainbow.

Princess paused the video.

'For context, this is when he was host of the popular 90s food-themed gameshow *Battered by the Butler*. It's an assault course where contestants make popular dishes while dodging evil butlers.'

Now it was my turn to spurt out Ribanta.

'*What?*'

'I know,' said Princess. 'It's basically *Ready Steady Cook* meets *Gladiators*. As if that would work!'

'I'd play it,' said Alicia.

'That's not what I meant,' I gasped. '*I* was just battered by a butler.'

'Oh,' said Princess. 'Did he look like this?' She fast-forwarded and paused on one of the butlers doing the battering. He and a dozen other butlers were trying to knock contestants off podiums into pools of gunk. He had more hair back then, but the face, glasses and magnified eyes were the same. I undid my bow tie to let some air in.

'Yes . . .' I wheezed. 'Yes . . . that's him.'

'Great!' said Princess. 'Then you'll recognise him in Japan. Our main suspect.'

'Don't worry, Col,' said Alicia. 'No one harpoons a Kingsley and gets away with it.'

'His name is Witherknife,' said Princess. 'This, by the way, is Lord Bobo today. He hasn't aged well.' A new slide clicked onto the screen. It showed a shabbier, flabbier, drabber Lord Bobo. His suit was sombre, rumpled and grey. His bowler hat sat skew-whiff, dented.

'Oh yeah,' said Princess. 'And he's now calling himself just *Mr* Bobo.'

'My head hurts,' said Alicia. 'We need to find a guy who is now a different guy and stop this other guy from harpooning this guy?'

'I guess you could phrase it like that,' said Princess.

'Can I just ask,' I said, reviving myself on Ribanta, 'why? I mean, why is Witherknife after Lord Bobo?'

Princess shrugged. 'It's your job to find out.' She went to a filing cabinet. 'Watch him. Watch those around him. Protect him. And don't forget to bow. It's big there.'

I muttered to Alicia, 'Maybe some kind of grudge? A pay dispute or something?'

'Soooo sorry to interrupt, guys,' cut in Pierce Aniseed, without sounding sorry at all, 'but maybe there's some kind of grudge. A pay dispute or something.'

'Great idea, Pierce,' said Princess. 'Anchovy,

something for you to pursue.'

'But I just said –'

'Someone from the Japanese G.S.L. will meet you in Tokyo. Which reminds me – your apprentice needs a provisional tattoo ASAP.'

Alicia fist-pumped.

'You should've done this already,' continued Princess, as Pierce Aniseed tutted in the background. 'She also needs a codename.'

'I was thinking my codename could be Allie Blaster?' said Alicia.

'I think,' said Princess, 'it might be an idea if I talk to your brother alone for a few moments, Alicia.'

Alicia went out – dropping a death stare on Pierce Aniseed – to find her squishy chair.

Pierce Aniseed closed the door behind her and coughed.

'Shall I read from the file, Princess?'

'No, Pierce, that won't be necessary.' She twisted

her ponytail into an even tighter knot. If that were possible. 'Now, Anchovy. I'm a *leetle beet* concerned about the trial case you mentored last week. Your apprentice almost drowning your geography teacher, specifically.'

'History teacher.'

'I don't care if he's teaching you home economics while riding a unicycle in a suit of armour. That was a ri*dic*ulous shish-up!'

'Do you want me to add "ridiculous shish-up" to the report, Princess?' butted in Pierce Aniseed. 'We've already logged "totally avoidable", "horrendous handling" and "fundamental fluff-up" as well as "mother of all –"'

'Let me finish, please, Pierce.' Princess thumbed a drum roll on her spatula-embossed ledger. 'Listen, Anchovy. You've got the job done before, in your own madcap way. And I'll admit it – as photographic-memory-guys go, you've got a lot to offer. But . . .'

There was the b-word. I knew it was too good to be true.

'When you're responsible for an apprentice, you need to be five steps ahead of them. Okay?'

'I understand, Princess. We'll be more careful.'

'Good. Now, we've got a long flight plus a layover ahead. I suggest you don't think about that bloodthirsty butler who just tried to maim you on a dark, muddy moor and who you'll have to follow once more in a foreign country. Just try to get some sleep.'

'Thanks.'

I found Alicia chatting to Yelena and Yaconda.

'Anata no . . . himitsu no tato~ū o . . . what was it? *Mite mo īdesu ka?'*

'You're a natural!' Yelena ruffled her hair. 'Your first phrase in Japanese!'

'What did you teach her?' I asked.

'It means, "Can you show me your secret tattoo?"' said Yaconda.

I hadn't even thought about trying to learn Japanese. Italian and Russian were hard enough.

Yelena threw me a mini phrase book. 'Better get that photographic memory in action, Anch.' I took a glance. Apparently there were *three* alphabets.

'Ja-paaaaaaann, babyyyyyyyyyyy!!!!!!!!!!!' whooped Alicia, kicking her little legs. Back when I joined the G.S.L., I remember how my head spun thinking about the places we'd go. Japan! It was the furthest I'd ever been. I thought of all the noodles I could slurp and chopsticks I would drop and cool cartoons I could watch. Alicia was practically horizontal in her lounger now. She whooped again.

'It's going to be greeeeaaaaaaaat!!!!'

Her enthusiasm was kind of infectious. Until I remembered the look on that butler's face.

Chapter 5

I de-gunked my sleepy eyes. As I was half in dreamland, what floated below seemed all the more spectacular. Honshu, the main island of Japan, was bathed in pink sun, with bottle-green shadows seeping over its crags. Lozenges of cloud waltzed in and out. Through these poked a mountain, its snowy peak blending with the lavender-blue clouds, painting the illusion of a mountain made *of* cloud, hovering above the land.

'Ooooooooooft!!' yelled my apprentice. 'This green toothpaste is hotttttttttttttttttttttttttttt!'

'That's because it's wasabi paste.' I snatched the tube. 'Your washbag's over there.'

We swooped around Tokyo Bay, gliding onto a runway that also materialised from nowhere.

'Tokyooooooo, babyyyyyyyyyyyyyyyyyyyyy!'

I made a mental note to hide all sugary treats from Alicia.

'*Sayonara*, you two,' said Yelena and Yaconda, saluting as we left the plane.

In the airport, Princess marched us through a booth that said 'For Diplomats'. She paused by the luggage carousel.

'Okay, you two. Do you want the bad news first or the good news?'

Guessing that the good news would still be fairly bad, and the bad news would be catastrophic, I didn't really care.

'The bad news,' said Princess, 'is that Witherknife will have people watching the airports.'

'Presumably you don't mean some nerdy plane spotters,' I said.

'No. I mean some local psychopaths with your photo and a grudge against backchat.'

'And the good news?'

'The good news,' whispered Princess, 'is that there's a secret escape train.'

'Where is it?' I asked, clocking Pierce Aniseed's mega-watt grin. Princess faced the black rubber fronds slapping against the suitcases as they emerged from the hole of the carousel.

'In there.'

'Har-har,' said Alicia. 'As *if*, Skewer!'

'It's *Princess* Skewer. You need to find the set of old-fashioned red suitcases with an elephant logo. Get inside them.'

'Did you say —'

'They're clipped together so you won't get separated. You've taken your Elementary

Contortion Grade One exam, so this should be straightforward.'

'What about you?' I asked Princess. 'Where are you going?'

'For security purposes, we must avoid travelling together. I'll be taking the Presidential Train.' She at least had the decency not to look smug. Unlike a certain Personal Assistant.

'Don't worry, guys!!' he mega-watted. 'I bet the G.S.L. Japanese suitcase-trains are the best in the world! Byeeeeeee.'

We were left staring into the recesses of the carousel. I grabbed Alicia's hand. 'Come on, Al.'

We watched the cases get spat in and out. It was slightly hypnotic; some were sparkly, some polka-dotted, some covered in ribbons. Two large red cases with shiny gold corners hummed around the bend. Handily, a ski-bag bearing the words *Lionpaw Towers* then toppled off. The crowd was distracted. I nudged Alicia.

'Now!'

We hopped onto the carousel, gripping the red cases, and slid through the hole. Up, down and all around us, suitcases chugged along, a giant game of airport snakes and ladders. Our conveyor belt was about to split. I flicked open the first case and helped Alicia with hers. To quote Princess, faffing was not an option.

If you've seen one contortion exam, you've seen them all. Face the nearest breathing hole, knees to the chin, spine in a nautilus-shell coil of pain, pain, pain. We wedged in and our cases turned off course, lurching down to a separate belt. At least they had a soft interior, with glowing buttons, a screen and headphones. These played an announcement in Japanese, then an American voice said, *'Welcome to G.S.L. Japan's Express Train Contortion Option. We will be arriving at your next destination in –* (pause) *– twenty-seven minutes –* (pause) *– and –* (pause) *– fourteen seconds. Please relax. We hope you will enjoy your journey with us.*' I suppose they had to say that last bit. At least I'd changed out of the tuxedo. A poor excuse for a breeze wafted through the breathing hole.

'You okay, Al?' I shouted.

'Greeeeeeeat,' came the reply, too muffled to know if it was sarcastic or not. We accelerated.

The combination of jet lag and nausea made me lose all grip on time. It may have been twenty-seven minutes and fourteen seconds, but it felt like a lifetime. Eventually, the tread of a conveyor belt was replaced by the irregular lug of human hands, hefting us onto a metal shelf.

More Japanese chirruped in the headphones, before the American robot translated: '*Welcome to your destination: Shibuya Station Lost Property Office. The carriage doors will open in a moment. Please wait.*'

The voice resumed after a pause. '*The security guard is visiting the restroom. Please vacate the suitcase immediately. Thank you and we hope to see you again very soon.*'

I edged out and saw an office lined with suitcases, umbrellas and forgotten soft toys. I released Alicia and immediately put a finger to my lips, remembering Princess's line about being five steps ahead. A toilet flush gave us our cue to hop it.

The station's office opened into an alley. A strip of grey sky rumbled above. There was drilling and someone playing lounge jazz. A white cat slinked in, its shadow in pursuit. We were opposite a small, orange-fronted restaurant, with bowls of soup in the window. Chopsticks pinching noodles hovered in mid-air, getting one up on gravity. I wasn't all that sure I was awake. My pizza watch beeped.

'When will I get one of those?' Alicia asked.

'Soon.' I read the message: **Tracking you. P.A.**

P.A. . . . Pah! Just the initials made me angry.

Head into the restaurant opposite, he buzzed again.

As we entered, a doorbell hummed like a barbershop quartet. We couldn't see any diners, but, curiously, we could *hear* them. The entire restaurant was full of half-open booths, which produced a chorus of slurping. Short slurps, long slurps, rapid-fire slurps and meandering slurps that got louder, then quieter, then louder again. And lots of 'aaaah' sounds. As we approached the booths, we saw the diners' heads burrowed in their bowls. Steam-clouds rose, tangling on the ceiling.

The pizza watch took another pinging from that Poser Assistant.

Sit at booth number fourteen. P.A.

What did it matter to him where we sat? Booth fourteen had a 'RESERVED' sign and a queue of people outside. Odd. Aniseed continued to spam us.

Jump the queue. P.A.

So now he was making us cheese off the locals. Great. I tried to say the word for 'sorry' from my phrase book:

'*Sumimasen, sumimasen . . .*'

We squeezed through and found a seat. The table had a hatch, where faceless hands whipped up a broth. This swam with noodles, seaweed, spring onions and a cloud-shaped slice of something white with a pink spiral in the middle. The menu translated this as being a 'fishcake'.

Another strange touch was that all around the booth hung bleached-out photos of movie stars, along with coloured fairy lights and strips of handwritten paper. I took a sachet of chopsticks and handed another to Alicia.

'Take these, Al . . . no, don't put them up your nostrils!'

'Col, there's some writing on the sachet . . .'

'Probably the name of the restaurant.'

'Actually, I think it's some secret message.'

I glanced at the sachet. My apprentice was right. It read: *Turn around and take off your sock and reveal your true identity, please!! Thank you!!* ☺

'Weeeeeeeiird,' chanted Alicia.

This would be weird for an apprentice. But not for a pro. I turned around. Staring into our booth was a girl in a navy trench coat, with hair curtaining half her face. She was with a small boy, who had rainbow-striped socks and the sort of cheeks that aunts like to squidge. I sighed, took off my trainer and sock, and splayed my toes to reveal

 my secret G.S.L. tattoo: a tiny Markus Anchovius, our Caesar

Pizza mascot, above a diamond of spatulas.

The girl's nostrils dilated, but she stayed strong and raised her hand. Then she pulled up her sleeve to reveal her own spatula-diamond tattoo, which was below a long-legged spider.

'*Ohayo gozaimasu!* Good morning, Detective Anchovy.' The girl smiled and gave a big bow. Her colleague's bow was even bigger. 'My name is Detective Monmon Miguomo, Japanese G.S.L. But you can call me just Monmon.'

The boy coughed.

'And this,' continued Monmon, 'is my apprentice, Norio.'

'Very nice to meet you both,' I said, and gestured to Alicia. 'Er, this is –'

'I was thinking my codename could be Wassup Wasabi?' said Alicia.

I let my face express what words couldn't.

'This is my apprentice,' I said.

'Can we come in?' said Monmon, squeezing into the booth with Norio.

The G.S.L. really like confined spaces. I've never understood it.

'Please tell me, Anchovy,' said Monmon, studying her black nail polish. 'What is the strangest thing about this booth?'

'The movie-star photos?' I tried.

Monmon shook her head.

'The fairy lights?' Alicia tried.

Now Norio shook his head.

'The strips of paper with handwriting?' I tried again.

Monmon shook her head vigorously.

'What then?' asked Alicia.

'The ceiling,' said Monmon, looking up.

'Uurgh!' said Alicia. 'Gross!'

'Is that –' I stared up at the ceiling '– what I think it is?'

Chapter 6

'*A fishcake*? On the ceiling?!'

It certainly looked like a fishcake on the ceiling: that cloud-shaped white slice with the pink spiral in the centre, stuck to the spot. Norio cleared his throat.

'It is not just any fishcake,' he said. 'This is a special fishcake with strange powers. The fishcake brings good luck. We call it –' he paused dramatically '– the *Good Luck Fishcake.*'

Alicia was glazing over. I couldn't blame her.

'I need an explanation,' I said. 'The Good Luck Fishcake?'

Monmon napkinned up a puddle of broth, then began. 'Years ago, a young man from a village outside Tokyo, with little money, came into this restaurant hungry and sad. He did what any sensible person would do. He ordered ramen.'

'Noodles.'

'Yes, ramen. He ate everything in the bowl, except he saved the *naruto* fishcake.'

'The what now?' said Alicia.

'The *naruto* fishcake,' said Monmon, 'is named after the famous Naruto whirlpools. Which is why it has this pink spiral shape.'

'Funkyyyyyyyyyyyyyy . . .' said Alicia. I nudged her.

'For Japanese children,' Monmon went on, 'this is a special symbol. When our teacher gives us a grade, they draw this symbol on our homework.'

She took out a sparkly gel pen and drew on a napkin.

'It is called a *hanamaru* symbol, but it is based on the Naruto whirlpools. It is the best grade you can get.'

'Ohhhh, nice,' I said. 'We get a gold star.'

'Interesting,' said Monmon. 'Anyway, this shape is seen as a symbol of success. Who knows? Maybe this is why the young man did something very strange.'

'What did he do?' I asked.

'He took the *narutomaki* in his hands,' continued Monmon, 'and he made a promise. He promised upon this fishcake that he will make his fortune.

And then –' Monmon pretended to throw something '– he threw it up on the ceiling! And it has been stuck there ever since!'

'Cool . . .' said Alicia, looking at the ceiling and reaching for her own slice of *naruto* fishcake.

'Don't even think about it,' I said, grabbing her wrist. Five steps ahead.

'Did he make his fortune then?' said Alicia.

'He has become one of the most famous men in Japan.' She pointed to one of the photos. It was a studio portrait of a man with a big collar, shiny hair and a cheeky smile. He looked like he had just heard an extremely funny and slightly rude joke.

'His name is Osamu Sato,' Monmon said. 'A very popular movie star.'

'And who are all the others?' I asked.

Monmon pointed at a lady in a sleeveless blouse and piled-up hair. She looked like she was laughing at a funnier, possibly slightly ruder joke.

'Her name is Kuniko Shinoi. She was also very poor. Somehow, she heard about this promise that Osamu Sato-sama made. And she decided to visit this restaurant. She looked at the *naruto* fishcake and made the same promise. Now she is a famous weather reporter.'

'Riiiiight,' I twigged. 'That's why you call it the Good Luck Fishcake.'

'The story is true of all these people,' said Monmon, indicating the celeb photos. 'They say they owe their fortune to this fishcake. Also,' she added, 'they say that should the fishcake ever fall, it will bring long life to the person who will catch it!'

'So these bits of paper,' said Alicia. 'They're wishes or prayers or something?'

'Correct,' said Monmon. 'People come to see the Good Luck Fishcake and make a wish that they shall become a star.'

'That's a great story,' I said, eager not to go *too*

off-grid. 'But, erm . . . how about, you know, Lord Bobo?'

'This is why we brought you here,' smiled Monmon. She whispered to Norio, who then shot off like an eel.

'This is the exact spot where Lord Bobo was last seen,' said Monmon.

'Oh! Any witnesses?'

Norio reappeared. He had brought over a short, broad woman in chef's overalls, a pointy white hat, salt-and-peppery hair and silver-rimmed glasses. She bowed. We bowed. I was beginning to get used to it.

'This is the owner of the restaurant,' said Monmon. I took out one of my favourite edible notebooks (tiramisu flavoured) and readied the pencil (also edible).

'What time did you last see Lord Bobo?' I asked.

Norio repeated the question in Japanese.

Monmon translated the answer.

'About 11:30. Not so busy, so there were not many people.'

'What was Lord Bobo doing?'

Norio asked, Monmon answered.

'He came here to pay his respects to the famous Good Luck Fishcake.'

'Was he alone?'

Yes, Norio and Monmon deduced. But, apparently, Bobo seemed nervous. The chef started gesturing, imitating Bobo. Turning his head. Toe-tapping. Twitching. In other words, the behaviour of a hunted man. The chef would have gone on further, but the barbershop-quartet doorbell hummed. Two sets of footsteps clicked in. One was light, the other heavy. I couldn't recognise the footsteps. But I could recognise one of the voices. It was very English. And very butlery.

'Bring her to me.'

The other person started giving orders in Japanese. I felt for my molten-tomato-purée gun. The footsteps grew louder. Monmon and Norio hadn't met Witherknife, but they knew the drill. Monmon produced her purée gun.

The footsteps were upon us. A shadow spread over the Good Luck Fishcake. Norio pressed into the wall. Alicia copied. The chef turned around and filled the entrance to our booth, forming a sort of chef-shield.

That voice from the old manor boomed again, accompanied by the rustle of paper.

'Is the man in this photo here, madam? Lord Bobo is his name.'

His companion translated. Some murmuring from our chef-screen.

'Oh. How disappointing,' the butler boomed. 'Be that as it may, madam, I want to look inside this booth.'

The chef knew her rights. I mean, it was mad enough that there were four people in there. Six would be Guinness World Record territory – you know, when thirty-four clowns bundle into a phone box or something. *Of course he couldn't come in*, I guessed the chef was saying. There was a paying customer in there.

'But I *need* to see this booth, madam!'

The chef-wall held out.

'I DEMAND TO SEE THIS BOOTH!'

Had he seen us? I held up the purée gun, trying to a) steady my heartbeat and b) hold Alicia's hand. Monmon looked cool. She held a finger to Norio's quivering lip.

'I DEMAND TO SEE THIS BOO–'

The battering butler stopped in his tracks. His Japanese companion placated him.

'Yes, yes, you're quite right, my dear Mystery Meats,' he purred.

Mystery Meats?

'Madam: we shall vacate your foul premises immediately.'

We heard the butler heel-spin and march off. Our chef-wall slid away, following him. We craned our heads out, just catching the black tailcoat flickering out of the door. The barbershop-quartet doorbell hummed again. We didn't see the so-called 'Mystery Meats'.

'Stay here,' said Monmon, and she slid out.

'No!' I whispered. 'That man is dangerous!'

'It's okay, Anchovy. He knows you, but not me.'

She was very casual. She hadn't been harpoon-gunned like I had. Norio looked up. Something was tickling his nose and getting in his eyes. Dust was pouring from above us and something was buzzing. Norio started coughing. Alicia spluttered. We charged out of the booth. Other diners stared. When the smoke cleared, I saw it: a neat hole in the ceiling. The Good Luck Fishcake was gone!

We pelted into the street. Where was Monmon? It was all too fast. A figure holding a colourful briefcase leapt from a window. Then it vanished through the sunroof of a van, emblazoned in red and blue. No one was in the alley, except the slinky white cat from earlier. I molten-puréed the van's back tyres, but only took out a taillight. I fired again. I missed again. The van rolled on.

'Stop!'

Monmon was trying to block the van. It didn't care. The hand on the wheel – white gloved – just drove on. Monmon went flying, tumbling into a nearby basement.

'Monmon!!' Norio cried. She was crumpled in a heap, groaning and bleeding from her head. We swept back her hair. I whipped off my trench coat and then my T-shirt, tearing it into strips. Norio and Alicia held them to her head. The white cat approached, mewling in concern.

Send an ambulance to my location, I typed to Pierce Aniseed on the pizza watch.

On its way, he returned. Good for something, at last. Rain began to spatter.

Chapter 7

'Why are you bare-chested?' someone snorted beneath an umbrella. It tilted back to reveal the finely chiselled features of Pierce Aniseed. I drew in my trench coat.

'Because, Aniseed, we used my T-shirt to bandage Monmon's cuts.'

'So there,' said Alicia.

Norio nodded. The <u>P</u>etty <u>A</u>ssistant just gave a *humph*. The white cat, which had stuck to Alicia like a magnet, hissed at him as we crossed the hospital car park. Pierce Aniseed opened the door

of a gleaming black car. In the front, with her
claw-shaped ponytail and pinstriped back to us, sat
Princess Skewer, simmering.

'That disgusting flea-ridden alley cat is *not*
coming in here.'

'His name is Bernard,' said Alicia, tucking the
cat under her arm and climbing in. Norio took the
other seat while Pierce Aniseed man-splayed in the
middle. This meant that I had to lie across them
like a wet, shirtless Roman emperor.

'Such a shame, guys, that Monmon broke her
arm,' sighed Pierce Aniseed as we set off. 'What are
the odds?'

I wiped the window, seeing that Alicia
had written a rude play on his name in the
condensation. Princess cleared her throat.

'I am beginning to wonder if there's some
sort of curse hanging over you, Anchovy.' She
began: 'I mean, the day you choose to visit a site

of local interest, there is a full-scale robbery! And somehow, for the second time this week, you let this not exactly well-camouflaged butler – yes, butler – GET AWAY!!'

I had no answer for that one.

'And how,' she went on, 'am I supposed to explain to the President of the Japanese G.S.L. that after working with us, their top detective winds up in A&E? Unbelievable! Just unbe-fluffing-lievable.'

We fell into silence. Why did everything I touch turn to disaster-dust? I gazed at wet Tokyo, wobbling beyond the glass. Bicycles made wave machines out of bloated puddles. A caterpillar of umbrellas bobbed along the pavement. We pulled up at a tower block whose ground-floor shop advertised beautiful papers, notebooks and ink brushes.

'So, guys,' said Pierce Aniseed, after conversing with the driver in immaculate Japanese. 'This area is called Jimbocho and is populated by bookshops. In this building, for example, all twelve floors are bookshops.' By the lift, a column of silver placards indicated the shops on each floor. The top one didn't have a placard – just a sellotaped sheet of paper, penned with: **スパチュラ・プレス・マンガ株式会社 (Spatula Press Manga Ltd)**.

Alicia asked Norio if she could press the button in the lift. Pierce beat her to it.

I avoided the scowling triple-Princess in the three-way mirror. We stepped out and gasped. It was an Aladdin's cave of comics – I should say manga – rammed from floor to ceiling. In fact, in the centre, you couldn't actually see the ceiling – it was stacked so high with what I can only describe as a *manga fortress*. Many were yellowing in plastic sleeves, with customers cooing over them like sacred relics.

Norio nodded to a father and daughter behind

the counter, then led us behind the manga fort. By a battered cover showing a superhero baseball player, he muttered, '*Aureum in spatha est, vivat in spatha.*' The manga slid back to reveal a wonky doorknob. Norio turned this, and a sizeable wodge of the manga-wall squeaked back to reveal an opening. He led us through, then up a ladder, through a hatch and into a hall, with polished bronze beams and sliding doors. Norio held out his arms.

'Welcome to the G.S.L. Tokyo branch.'

'We'll be stationed here, Anchovy,' said Princess. 'Try not to burn the place down this time.'

Norio indicated a neat line of slippers for us to put on. Princess and her PA went off for some 'conference calls' and Norio took us along the corridor and made us change into *another* pair of slippers. Then we entered one of the small, paper-walled rooms. Inside was a boy with a cartoon-splash-shape of black hair, a white lab coat and a green blob exiting his left nostril.

'Camillo!' I said and gave him a hug.

'Anchovy!' I hoped he hadn't deposited the green blob on me.

'This is Camillo,' I said to Alicia. 'The G.S.L. Inventor.'

'Oh yeah!' said Alicia, putting down Bernard. 'I remember your X-ray torch from my training mission in the woods. You should've seen my brother's pants!'

'Ah, well,' said Camillo, 'it is not really for looking at the underwear of people, but for seeing special locks and hidden switches.'

'This is my apprentice,' I said. 'Her name's . . . uh . . .'

'I was thinking my codename could be Noodle Caboodle?'

'Pleased to meet you,' said Camillo politely.

Norio coughed and pointed to some gym mats

on the floor, which it turned out were beds. The room also contained Alicia's double-bass case – minus her double bass, now I think about it. Norio bowed and left us.

'So what brings you here, Cam?'

'Well –' he unzipped his suitcase – 'the G.S.L. have an exchange programme for inventors. So I am here, and there is a Japanese inventor in London. Or Rome, I cannot remember. It is amazing here! Anyway, I have some gadgets for you two.'

He brought out a pair of pointy leather shoes from the suitcase. More footwear?

'Aw, thanks, Camillo!' said Alicia. 'I need a new pair of school shoes!'

'Actually, it is not a good idea to wear these at school,' said Camillo, 'because they are irons.'

'Irons?' I said.

'Yes.'

'As in, irons?'

'Yes, underneath they are red-hot irons.' He held up the metal soles. 'Click your heels together three times to turn them on,' said Camillo, 'and four times to turn them off.' He demonstrated and the soles began smouldering. 'These are good for defending against attackers or breaking down doors.'

'Or just getting creative with ironing shirts,' I said.

'Yes,' said Camillo. 'Interesting British humour. Also . . .' He reached into the box of tricks again and brought out two new molten-purée guns, giving one to Alicia.

'Coooooool!!!'

'Ah, yes, please be careful. It is hot like lava and

can scald, blind or maybe cause some memory loss to your attacker.'

'Cooooooool!!!'

Camillo shot me a glance. I moved her arm down and away from us. Camillo carried on.

'Here tomato is not so common, so we use the, ah . . . sour plum, yes. Now press the green button and then –'

He was interrupted by a *NEEEOWWWWWW-WWWWW* and a sizzling sound in the paper door. Bernard leapt ten feet.

'Woah, that button is seriously sensitive!'

'Al, for the love of crust be careful with that purée gun! These walls are literally paper thin!'

'Yes, please be careful,' said Camillo. 'Also, I brought this for you, Anchovy.'

He produced a small jar of capers, which was kind. No anchovy pizza is complete without these salty green gems.

'Yum, thanks, Cam.'

'Ah . . . you must not eat these, please, Anchovy.'

'What are they, ultra-mini hand grenades?'

'No, but this is a good idea,' said Camillo dreamily. 'No, I call these "capercorders".'

'Caper-whats?'

'Capercorders. In general, these are tracking devices . . . ah, I think you say "bugs" in English.' He produced a kind of peashooter. Or capershooter. 'You can shoot the capercorder and it will be stuck to someone, so you can follow their movements from your pizza watch.'

I pulled a capercorder from the jar. It was super sticky. There was also an orange dot pulsing inside it. A corresponding dot flashed on my watch and a teeny map of the base appeared.

'Wow.'

Camillo shrugged. 'There is another gadget you can use also: a special turbo-charged pogo stick.

You need to –'

'Having fun with your toys, guys?'

Pierce Aniseed stood beaming in the doorway. He then turned around to examine the hole made by the purée gun. I don't know what got into her, but Alicia grabbed the capershooter and pinged a capercorder at the back of Pierce Aniseed's head! Anyone else and I might have told her off. He spun around peevishly.

'Detective Anchovy, the boss would like to see you.'

'Princess Skewer, you mean?'

'No. I mean the President of the Tokyo G.S.L.'

'Am I in trouble?'

'We'll soon find out!'

Alicia puffed out her cheeks. 'Deny everything, Col. I mean – Anchovy.'

I followed Pierce out and along the corridor. He pointed to a ladder. Once I was through the hatch, he shut a trapdoor behind me, leaving me standing in a metallic booth with rows of tiny holes. A loudspeaker suddenly announced something in Japanese, which an American robot voice translated as, '*Welcome to the G.S.L. Japan bathhouse. Before entering, we kindly ask you to please remove all items of clothing.*'

What??!!

Was I summoned here because I stank? A hatch opened and the loudspeaker announced again, after the Japanese, '*We kindly ask you to deposit all clothing in the container provided.*' I sighed. Sometimes questioning the G.S.L.'s methods just slows things down.

I rolled up my clothes, along with my pizza watch. Before I could work out where the water would come from, I got the answer: everywhere. It was like being in a carwash. Jets shooting out from all sides, power-hosing my skin. Then a jet of soap blasted into my midriff.

'*We kindly ask you to close your eyes,*' said the cooing American robot voice. More soapy jets fired at my arms, my legs, my face . . . you get the idea. The droning increased, and two massive spongey cylinders began rolling over me. Metal arms then lowered scrubbing brushes, which whirred and pumped, heavy on the pores. More jets of water blasted.

I waited for the assault-by-washing to die down. It took a while. Bubbly trails drained away. Warm air blasted in, along with a puff of Japanese talcum powder. A door slid open.

'*Please step this way.*' More robot instructions. I went into a small room, flanked with warm wooden slats. I put on the dressing gown and rubber shoes left there. A door bore a plaque with the diamond of spatulas, below a skull and a key.

'*The boss will see you now,*' the robot cooed.

Chapter 8

Japan had been pretty weird so far. And it had just got a whole lot weirder. I was in a vast, misty room tiled in a hundred shades of green. Light oozed in from small stained-glass panes near the ceiling. A creaky pulley ushered in a line of towels. Oh, and the boss was in a bubble bath. Also – the bubbles were *gold*.

'*Konbanwa*,' I said with a bow, picturing page five of the Japanese phrase book. 'You wanted to see me?'

'Mark Anchovy! Come a little closer.'

I perched on a ledge by a tray strewn with the remnants of lunch. The boss of the Tokyo branch had a shaved head, a slim face and the ghosts of a few spots. He took the top block from a miniature pyramid and dropped it into the bath, puffing up more gold bubbles. 'Gold-leaf bath bomb,' he said, with a smooth English accent. 'A speciality from the region of Kanazawa. Anyway, since I know your name, I should introduce myself. My name is Skeleton Key.'

I reeled and stared into his eyes. One was blue, the other brown.

'I think,' he continued, rolling those eyes, 'that you knew my brother: your original mentor – Master Key.'

'Yes!' I said, recalling that Master Key had Japanese family. 'Master Key was such a help; he was a great boss to me.'

'I don't want to talk about him,' Skeleton Key cut in. He gazed into the bubbles. 'Mr Perfect. Do you know how many times I've had to listen to people praise him? The best boss. The biggest cases. The most famous friends. The biggest G.S.L. branch.'

'London's got the biggest branch?'

'Well, after the Swiss branch, of course, which is the mothership, but you knew that.'

I didn't know that.

Skeleton Key pressed a flannel to his head. 'Oh, it's already starting to hurt . . . I shouldn't have brought him up.'

'I didn't know Master Key had a brother.'

'Well, we don't speak very much, so I don't know why you would.' He splashed and sighed. 'Ahhh. I shouldn't get angry, it's not good for me. But I wanted to talk to you.'

'Because I'm in trouble?'

'No, you're not in trouble. I like you, Anchovy. There's something we have in common.'

'Master Key, you mean –'

'Please!' He closed his eyes. 'I don't want to talk about him. No. There is something else.'

I wasn't into gold-leaf bath bombs, so it couldn't have been that.

'Do you get headaches, Anchovy?'

'Yes, I do, especially when I'm remembering stuff.'

'I know. Because I, too, have a photographic memory.'

'Oh, wow. Cool!'

'Anchovy – trust me, it's not cool. It's fun at first, but when your memories keep on piling up it just becomes . . .' He clenched his fists and crushed a bath bomb, as a phone by the soap dish began to trill. Skeleton Key answered it with the same curtness that he used when talking about his brother, now switching to Japanese.

'Why is everything such a hassle?' he moaned, putting down the phone. 'Why should I come down to supper later? I mean, I've got so much I need to get done here!' He flung *another* bath bomb in. The gold bubbles were threatening to form a sort of foamy igloo. With the time he'd spent in there, he must've been wrinklier than my granddad, G-pops.

'What did you want to see me about?' I asked.

'Today's robbery . . .' he said. 'I want to test this famous memory of yours – there aren't many photographic-memory detectives around these days. What did you notice about the getaway vehicle?'

'The number plate? Oh, that's easy —'

'Anchovy, let's skip the rookie-level stuff, shall we? Of course you'd remember a number plate, but as any basic burglar knows, those number plates will now be replaced and disposed of . . .' He patted his face with the flannel. 'What else did you notice?'

I sat back and closed my eyes. I rewound the mental film footage of the attack in the alley. There was the van. The figure jumping through the sunroof, clutching the briefcase. Annoyingly, I could clearly see this briefcase — which was pink with green checks — but not the owner of said briefcase. The shadow of the alley had drowned their face, so it appeared only as a silhouette:

'I didn't get a face shot of one of them,' I said to Skeleton Key. 'But . . .' I remembered the white glove on the wheel. And freezing that film still, I saw the face in the wing-view mirror.

'The driver was Witherknife.'

'Hardly surprising. What else?' said Skeleton Key. 'More, I need more.'

Bath bombs or information? I guessed information. I froze the film still as the van lurched at Monmon.

'There was a tiny piece of paper flying around.'

'And?'

I zoomed into the film still – to the paper fluttering alongside Monmon's purée gun.

'It was stamped in blue ink . . . looks like some sort of ticket.'

'What's on the ticket?'

I zoomed in further. 'A number.'

'What else?'

Zoom, zoom. I was reaching blurring point on the Colin Camera.

'A logo . . .'

'What of?'

'It's . . . an octopus . . . in a tie and a bowler hat. And some Japanese characters.'

'Can you copy them on the back of that napkin on the tray? You'll find a pen there.' I took the napkin and copied it, badly.

'Hmmmm. Not the sort of thing you could make up . . . good remembering. Now, hold on . . .' He massaged his temples and sank into the bubbles so just the top half of his head appeared, like a crocodile. He blew up more bubbles. Then resurfaced.

オクトボールズ
株式会社

'This ticket, judging from the markings, is a parking ticket for a factory car park. This is on . . . Let me just try to get up the city map . . .'

I couldn't believe this . . . could he really hold so gigantic a city as Tokyo in his brain? Skeleton Key did his crocodile-impression again, breathing heavily into the bubbles, his eyes closed. He surfaced, wincing a little.

'Yes . . . ah, yes . . . I can see it now. It's on Matsuura Street. I've seen a sign with this logo there before. Tomorrow you and your apprentice need to go to the factory.'

'What's the factory called?'

'Octoballs Limited. They used to make *takoyaki* – these are balls of fried octopus, green onions, bits of tempura batter, other things, a kind of brown sauce, but anyway. My guess is that the Good Luck Fishcake has been taken there.'

'Wow.'

'Wow yourself, Anchovy. We'd make a good team if I didn't have to be a boss. Oh, can you take down my tray? And please tell them I'm not coming down to supper. Sushi! Urgh!'

'Er, okay,' I said and got up. 'Nice to meet you.'

'You too, Anchovy. Good work . . . and good luck tomorrow.'

'Thanks.'

I left via the shower room, the trapdoor and the ladder. Weirder and weirder.

Back in the bedroom, Alicia spun around, stroking Bernard.

'Ah, Mr Anchovy . . . I've been expecting you.'

'Were you?' I asked.

'Naaah, not really, just thought I'd say that. How was the boss?'

'Bubbly. How was the rest of the gadget briefing?'

'I got a fancy pastille watch, look!' She held up

what looked like a band of Fruit Pastilles wrapped around her wrist. The black pastille folded up to reveal a special G.S.L. watch face. It also had the latest in-built camera and a laser function. Way cooler than mine. As long as she remembered it was a watch and not an actual Fruit Pastille. I thought back to Skeleton Key and Master Key, and then back to Alicia. I mean, yes, she ate important alibis, and nearly drowned my history teacher, and was currently trying to feed wasabi paste to Bernard, but still – I couldn't imagine not speaking to her.

'I was thinking maybe my codename could be Fruity P?'

'Not bad,' I said.

A dinner gong donged. I opened the sliding wall – the hole Alicia had made now indiscreetly gaffer taped – and found Norio in the corridor.

'Nice hanten,' he said, pointing at my dressing gown.

We followed him up into a glass-walled dining room at the very top of the building.

The night-lights of Tokyo pulsated around us. A long table was surrounded by a model railway track, sprouting from a hidden kitchen below. A white, bullet-nosed train whizzed around the track, carrying pastel-coloured plates of sushi. Princess Skewer and her pesky PA were tapping a button to make the train stop at their place. And there was poor Monmon! Her arm was in plaster. We rushed over and asked how she was. She was pleased to see us and pleased to see Bernard, who was following Alicia around like a shadow. Alicia asked Monmon if she could sign her plaster cast, which she agreed to. She took out a fat blue marker and wrote:

GET WELL SOON MONMON!!!!
BIG LOVE FRUITY P. X X X X X

There was an empty place at the head of the table, presumably for Skeleton Key. I grabbed two powder-pink plates off the sushi train. They contained two pucks of rice, wrapped in seaweed, with shiny yellow gunk on top.

'That's called uni,' said Monmon.

'Smells like a mermaid's armpit,' muttered Alicia.

'It is actually a sea urchin,' said Monmon.

'Holy wholegrain!' shouted Pierce Aniseed, rummaging through his shampoo-advert curls. 'Which one of you pizza-delivering pests threw a caper in my hair?'

'That's very presumptuous, Pierce,' I said, elbowing my apprentice. 'Just because we work for a pizzeria it doesn't mean we throw capers.'

'Humph . . . well, changing the subject, how was your little trip to see the boss, Anchovy?' He beamed like an overly zealous lighthouse. 'I hope you didn't get into trouble?'

'No, actually,' I said, pincering the *uni*. 'We

just hung out. And I learnt some very useful information for the investigation.'

'Humph,' he snorted again.

Anchovy: One. Aniseed: Nil.

Chapter 9

Some people wake to birdsong, others to fresh coffee. I awoke to something burning.

Charred footprints were smouldering all over the floor. Alicia had tipped a vase of water onto them. Bernard mewled.

'What happened?'

'It's a design flaw of the iron-shoes. I thought I'd turned them off, but it's *super* unclear.'

'I thought Camillo said you just click your heels together three times to turn them on, and four times to turn them off, no?'

'I lost count.'

I turned to the mentor's logbook and in the Catalogue of Apprentice Misdemeanours and Offences wrote, 'Nearly set fire to the host HQ.' Then again, I remembered that I'd had similar run-ins. Perhaps it ran in the family.

'We've got a lot of investigating to do today, Al – maybe you should just put on your normal shoes.'

'But the normal shoes won't help us break down any doors, will they, Col? Come on, it won't happen again, I promise! Let's try them out – it'll be fun!'

I sighed and picked up my own iron-shoes. Everyone at breakfast had got up way before us. Monmon's plaster cast was now covered in signatures and get-well-soon messages. Norio sat beside her, in blue overalls, matching cap and his trademark socks. Camillo was fixing the sushi train. I had to take a grilling from Princess about the iron-shoe mishap. Then I had to tell Alicia that, no, they didn't have Honey Nut Loops and if she didn't like the fishy broth and rice, then tough. She liked her bubble tea, though.

'Remind me, Anchovy,' said Princess. 'Which part of Tokyo are you wrecking today?'

'We need to investigate a factory complex called Octoballs Limited.'

'Because?'

'Because there's a stolen lucky fishcake there.'

Princess sighed and got up. 'I won't ask. Come on, Pierce.'

She left to do whatever it is that G.S.L. branch presidents do, and Pierce Aniseed left to do some squat thrusts in the G.S.L. gym. Us run-of-the-mill detectives set out, with Bernard in tow. A new day. Hopefully a better day. The black car was waiting for us.

I loved watching Tokyo. I saw a group of schoolchildren with uniforms like sailor suits. I saw a police station that seemed to have a moat around it. I saw some outdoor table tennis, with a guy using a saucepan instead of a racket. I saw two dogs wearing Cub Scout uniforms. Less lovable was Octoballs Factory, which, like most factories, was a soulless, blocky compound, full of crates and the honk of sewage. Even the octopus logo was ugly. We waited in the car outside the gates. Norio got out first, holding a clipboard. Monmon made us wait and tapped her G.S.L. watch. I think it was shaped like a dumpling. A *gyoza*? Norio went over to a security booth.

'Anchovy,' said Monmon, 'is it possible to ask Camillo if he can hack into the security cameras, and then replace today's footage with yesterday's footage?'

'He can do that in his sleep,' I said, tapping into my pizza watch.

Norio was showing his clipboard to a security guard who badly needed a haircut.

'Get ready to follow me, please,' said Monmon.

At that moment, a huge lorry swerved into the forecourt. Norio waved it over. Its number plate bore a tiny diamond of spatulas. The security guard scratched his head. I think he also needed a hair *wash*, come to think of it. The lorry halted, beeping and tooting. Then a kid in blue overalls, like Norio's, sprang out of the lorry and offloaded a crate. Then another kid in overalls did the same. And another. The crate supply seemed to go on forever.

A second, equally dopey security guard walked over. The crates kept coming, multiplying like spores. The ~~snooze patrol~~ security guards were getting agitated. Pretty soon there was a crate pile to rival Mount Fuji. And this crate pile formed an effective wall to be stealthy behind.

My pizza watch pinged.

The cameras are no longer working — Camillo.

'Okay, guys,' said Monmon. 'Let's go. When I start shouting, enter the factory.'

'Can Bernard come?' asked Alicia. But Monmon was already outside, opening the car boot and pulling out a small, bent bicycle. A third security guard was peering at Norio. He didn't look as sleepy. He looked suspicious. Monmon wheeled over the broken bike. We followed, keeping hidden behind the crates. The third security guard began barking questions. He'd smelt something. Something other than sewage. On the plus side, he'd vacated the door to the main building. Monmon started shouting at Norio. She was gesturing to him, the lorry, her broken bike, her broken arm. She was creating another layer of distraction. We were arrowing over the threshold when Bernard decided to introduce himself with a meow. The third security guard turned towards our position. Norio resorted to the ultimate trump card: crying.

'*MAAAAAAAAAAAAAAAAAAAAAAAAH!*'

It was a third layer of distraction. A sort of distraction-lasagne. We bolted through the door.

'Now what?' whispered Alicia.

'Erm . . .'

I hadn't even thought about the hard part: trying to find a particular fishcake in a particularly big factory.

'Let's go this way,' I guessed. We followed a dim corridor, lined with doors bearing the ugly

Octoballs logo. I peeped through the doors'
portholes. There were people shuffling papers,
people watering pot plants, people flirting by
vending machines. Nothing special. But the last
door was different.

'Holy mackerel!'

'What is it?' moaned Alicia, tapping her feet.

I've seen some weird things in my time with
the G.S.L. A mini–submarine below the Trevi
Fountain. A toilet that could fly. Gold–leaf bath
bombs. To name just a few. But what I was seeing
might have won first prize for world's weirdest.

Chapter 10

It was a shrine to Lord Bobo. I say 'shrine' because the walls of this room were plastered from floor to ceiling with photos of him. And photos from all angles: front on, profile, full length, quarter length, close-ups on his hands, his feet, his mouldy old clothes, his mouldy old moustache. He really had let himself go.

The occupant of the office was staring at the photos and – get this – *stroking* them. She had her back to us, so I could only see her light-beige suit, long dark hair and black gemstone earrings. Was this Bobo's GF? And why was she harbouring a stolen Good Luck Fishcake?

Stupidly, I'd forgotten to set the pizza watch to silent. A message beeped from Monmon. The corridor seemed to amplify the beep by a hundred.

Anchovy, what is going on?

I ducked away from the porthole. I heard Bobo's secret admirer step towards the door. *What's going on is that we've just been busted*, I wanted to write. The doorhandle turned.

Now, Princess was obviously not a Bernard-fan. But he clearly had his uses. As the woman left her Bobo Shrine, she didn't see the two trench-coated English kids pressed behind the door, but she did see the white cat darting in the opposite direction. She followed him around the corner.

We waited a few seconds, then crept after her. She chased Bernard out of a back door, making noises that maybe meant 'shooo!' in Japanese. I put a hand over Alicia's mouth to muffle her cries of 'Bernard!!' The back door led to a courtyard with cars, motorbikes and a large shed with corrugated metal walls.

Beige Suit Lady had given up the Bernard-hunt and was heading shed-wards. The door didn't have a porthole. There weren't even windows. Unless you counted the postage stamp of glass near the top. Our target went in. We heard the door bolt shut. Bernard saw us and leapt into Alicia's arms. She covered him in unhygienic smooches.

'Al,' I said, 'you like climbing, right?'

'What do you want me to do?'

'Can you get up to that little square window and see what's inside?'

'What will I get in return?'

'Er, something positive in the mentor's logbook? For a change . . .'

She frowned, put down Bernard and scanned the wonky drainpipes.

'I've got an idea,' she said, and marched to a nearby scooter. With a force of strength that both impressed and horrified me, she wrenched off its wing mirror.

'Alicia Kingsley!' I hissed, adopting the parent voice. It had the reverse effect. She now wrenched off the *other* wing mirror. Even Bernard seemed shocked.

'All under control,' she said nonchalantly, almost humming the words. I took out my mentor's logbook and turned to the Catalogue of Apprentice Misdemeanours and Offences. Next to today's date, I simply wrote: 'VANDALISM'.

I'd barely finished underlining it when she began climbing up my back like I was a human tree, instead of her older brother and G.S.L. mentor. Her boots boshed me in the shoulder blades and her mini-mitts covered my eyes.

'What are you doing?'

'Col, can you keep still, please?!'

She handed me a butchered wing mirror. Then, using my head as a sort of launchpad, she vaulted onto the drainpipe. As I've mentioned, she was a master climber. She started shinning up towards the little square window.

'Be careful!'

'Meh,' I heard her reply. 'Wowzah.'

'What can you see up there?' I whispered.

'That's what the mirrors are for – we can use them like a periscope!'

She held her mirror at an angle to the opening. I was impressed. I re-opened the mentor's logbook and put an asterisk next to 'VANDALISM'. At the bottom I added 'for a good cause'. Then I lined up my mirror with Alicia's.

'What the . . .' I heard Alicia gasp, up on the

drainpipe. In my mirror, I saw what she saw: tables of workers with vats of water and tubs of chemicals. I could see Beige Suit Lady's face now – taut, smiling, with flushed cheeks and colourful braces. She was talking to a worker – a young woman in a bandana. This worker poured green sludge into the water and sloshed it around. The sludge seemed to harden and crinkle. The worker palmed it, then grabbed the corners and nursed out a green sheet. Then she tore it in two. She scrunched one half into a ball and wrapped the other around it. It was my turn to gasp. She had made a perfectly formed fake cabbage.

She placed this on a tray of other fake cabbages. Well, I'm guessing they were fake. I wouldn't eat them if they were real anyway. Cabbages . . . urgh. Alicia swung the mirror and we surveyed other workers, also sloshing chemicals into water and sculpting them as they crinkled. They were making everything. Sushi, glistening soups, hard-boiled eggs, chopped greens, pieces of salmon, balls of rice, things in batter, wrinkly mushrooms. All fake. It was like magic. And mouth-watering.

I set my pizza watch to silent and tapped a reply to Monmon: **They've got tons of pictures of Lord Bobo and make fake cabbages. Weird.**

She replied: **This is called sanpuru and is very popular in Japan. Restaurants use plastic food in their windows to show customers what is inside. It is normal. The photos of Lord Bobo are less normal.**

Arigato, I replied.

We are tracking you, wrote Monmon. **Good luck!!**

Alicia tilted the mirror back onto Beige Suit. She was with someone else now. Because of the angle we couldn't see their face. But we didn't need to. We saw his pinstripes. His waistcoat. His white gloves. And with these, he was clutching that pink-and-green checked briefcase. Very possibly with that Good Luck Fishcake inside. Beige Suit was listening intently. She looked worried. She nodded. She gulped. Who wouldn't? If Bobo was her BF, then this butler was about to burst her bubble. Was he threatening her? To get to Bobo? But why the

Good Luck Fishcake? He finished his lecture and headed for the shed door. Before I could say 'get down from your spy-post' to Alicia, I heard the bolt snap back.

Chapter 11

itherknife crossed the courtyard, the briefcase in tow. I crouched behind a scooter, praying that he wouldn't spot the G.S.L. apprentice perched up near the windowsill.

Witherknife is threatening Bobo's GF, I typed to Monmon and the team. **And he's got the fishcake.**

The battering butler approached a surprisingly cutesy, clownish car.

Camillo typed back: **Ciao, Anchovy, I think now is a good time to use the capercorder!**

Good idea! ☺ wrote Monmon. **Can you use this, please?**

I felt for the capershooter and loaded up one of Camillo's caper-bugs.

I peeked over the scooter and made a thumbs up to Alicia, still clinging to her drainpipe like a peevish koala. She scowled back. I then focused on Witherknife's tailcoat, hoped for the best and fired. It pinged off his earlobe. He spun. I ducked. I waited for his butler boots to resume crunching. I peeked up again, my hand quivering. He unlocked the clown-car. I fired again. This time the caper-bug was nowhere near. I think it ended up in a tree. *Come on, Colin*, I willed myself. *Focus.* I fired again. A second before the car door shut, I saw a little green dot clinging onto the briefcase. Bullseye. The clown-car revved off.

'Er . . .' called Alicia from her spy post. 'Can I come down now?'

'The sooner the better, Al.'

Right on cue, the black G.S.L. car rolled
into the courtyard and we hopped in. Norio had
changed into a black waistcoat, white shirt and
bow tie. Monmon was peering at her *gyoza* watch.

'Incoming video call from Princess Skewer-san,'
she said. 'For everybody.'

I took a deep breath and opened my pizza
watch. Alicia opened her pastille watch.

'*Konichiwa*, everybody,' said Princess,
appearing on our watches.
'Right. We'll make sure
that every delegate in every
restaurant, kiosk and food cart in
Tokyo is monitoring Octoballs Limited from now
on. Good job.'

I exhaled, finally.

'We're tracking the capercorder: Witherknife
is heading to a contemporary art gallery called

TAFKAR. TAFKAR stands for The Artist Formerly Known As Rat, a celebrity artist. Apparently, he's got some big show opening tonight. He's a total rip-off of someone way better, by the way.'

'What's the plan, Skewer?' said Alicia.

'It's *Princess* Skewer.' Amazing how she could radiate displeasure even on a watch screen. 'Monmon will watch the front,' she went on. 'Norio will be stationed at the canapé table. We have a delegate in the gallery café if you need some props – she's called Mimi and has dark hair with a blonde braid. I suggest you find some canapés and distribute them. No one's expecting you to know anything about the art, don't worry, Anchovy – just keep an eye on that maniac manservant. Any questions?'

'Will there be any free food?' said Alicia.

'Perhaps I didn't phrase that properly,' said Princess. 'Any *real* questions?'

Alicia frowned into her pastille watch.

'No?' said Princess. 'Okay then – over and out.'

Eventually, we pulled up at a building shaped like a toppled stack of LEGO. Monmon guarded the door. In the lobby, a canapé crew were serving people in dark suits and blue-tinted sunglasses. Norio introduced us to the blonde-braided Mimi. I coughed, then got Alicia to form a sort of screen while I went through the humiliating sock-removal routine.

'You know,' sighed Alicia, holding her nose, 'a wrist or finger tattoo would be so much better.'

Mimi did the standard eyebrow-raising nod of recognition, then handed us some trays of canapés.

'Don't touch them,' I said to Alicia. We went into the cavernous gallery, following the stampede of suits as they swarmed around a man wearing a backwards flat cap and red-tinted sunglasses. The Artist Formerly Known As Rat. Or TAFKAR to you and me. Camera flashes captured him on his wave of devotion. Were we not having to save a cranky Brit from potential butler assassination, I might have enjoyed the gallery. It was full of these eye-popping mirror-dotted sculptures you could walk inside. Some of the sculptures – of things like elephants, mushrooms or giant eyeballs – were inflatable, which looked fun.

What with this riot of colour, the camera flashes and all the kookily dressed artists – not to mention the sledgehammer of jet lag – it was hard to adjust my vision and search for Witherknife. But we got him. Briefcase in hand, he was heading to a giant dotted snail at the far end of the gallery.

Alicia had dropped a canapé and was mopping gunk off the floor. I followed and tried to stay hidden behind the hedge of hipsters. It's hard to imagine someone so blocky vanishing, but Witherknife managed it. On approaching, it became clearer: the giant snail was hollow. I hesitated, recalling the encounter on the moor and the attack on Monmon. But business was business. I clasped one hand around the purée gun inside my coat and entered the snail shell.

Inside, a hundred circular mirrors volleyed coloured light back and forth. An ultramarine-blue light invaded most of the space. There were pillars and alcoves and the swirl of the shell's walls. I caught the sound of whispering. But there was no Witherknife. A light pattering announced someone of a very different build. I turned to see the artist in the red-tinted glasses. He was holding Witherknife's briefcase.

He took a step towards me and flashed his grotty teeth.

'We have an expression, in Japanese,' he began, 'that when the mongoose is too curious, the rat will bite the mongoose.' Not really an expression,

I suppose, more of just a fun fact about the animal kingdom. The artist lowered his red sunglasses. 'I am sure you have heard of me, little boy,' he continued. 'Because everybody has heard of TAFKAR: The Artist Formerly Known As Rat.'

The blue light inside the shell now turned to purple and then to red. The mirror-dots seemed to pulse.

'And you, little boy,' continued Ratface, 'are a mongoose.' Not the most accurate metaphor – my codename was Mark Anchovy, not Mark Mongoose. He delved into his jacket and brought out a lead pipe. As he whirled it above his head, I wasn't so sure he really *was* an artist. Bringing out my purée gun, I fired a laser jet of molten hot plum-paste right at his sternum. The result of this was a supernova of glass shattering in all directions. I just had time to clock that I had fired at a mirror, before the light that was now morphing from red to orange to green finally faded and all went black.

Chapter 12

The day, if you remember, had begun with something burning. It was now ending with something freezing. That something was a beaten-up pizza detective, tied and gagged inside a deep storage-chest freezer. Those of you who have followed my previous casework might remember that I've been in deep storage-chest freezers before, only they have magically morphed into G.S.L. shuttle trains. This didn't feel like one of those freezers.

No. This was a genuine freezer, giving me genuine pneumonia. My hands were a shade of

Smurf-blue. Bags of what might have been squid rings or fish fingers – it's not important – were wedged beneath me. At least they might have reduced the swelling on the gobstopper-sized lump on my head. I shouted through my gag. It came out as the pathetic muffle I knew it would. I kicked the end of the freezer.

DOOOOOOOM!

This didn't yield any results either. Through the ropes I saw my pizza watch; the screen was cracked and frozen over. Nobody knew where I was. Alicia! Had the delegates helped her get back to the base? I kicked the end of the freezer again.

DOOOOOOOM!

Nothing. Absolutely nothing. Just a glaring industrial drone and the swirling white noise of my icy prison. So this was it – the untimely end of Colin Kingsley AKA Mark Anchovy. What had I done to show for myself? I had found a stolen painting in Rome, some missing jewelled egg cups in Moscow, but there could've been more, so much more . . . I kicked again.

DOOOOOOOM!

Wait a minute. Why was I being so stupid? The iron-shoes! Gagged and bound, I could still click my heels together. Within seconds they were steaming, and two shoe-shaped holes were seared into the wall of the freezer, giving off an acrid whiff. I pressed in, harder.

The heat had melted the ice on the lid into a giant shower, but it was at least reviving me. The wall began to warp as I kicked, gathering strength like a racehorse in a tantrum. I kicked again, harder. There was another _DOOOOOOOM!_ And then a _KREEEEEEEEK_ as a screw squeaked from its moorings.

A chink of light appeared. I kicked again and the whole side came whistling off, sliding me, a few gallons of water and twenty packs of squid rings/fish sticks/tuna steaks onto a tiled floor.

Still bound, I could at least sit up now. I was in a kitchen storeroom, which was thankfully empty. Two big silver fridges were droning, horribly. They sounded worse than our duffed-up fridge in Caesar Pizza.

I pressed the rope on my wrists against the iron-shoes, again and again, until it had melted to shreds. The rope on my feet was a doddle. The tape on my mouth was painful. I stood up, using a food trolley for support, a free detective. For now.

There were no henchmen in sight, but something wasn't right. The droning. It had gone from horrible to deafening. As I turned to the source, two red lights glowed on each fridge. I noticed that the fridges had small treads underneath them, like you get on tanks. And now, in perfect sync, the doors of the fridges opened. I wondered if they were . . . but before I could think the phrase 'robotic fridges', two machine-gun barrels poked out from where the salad trays should have been.

I darted behind the food trolley. Blasting in my direction, they sounded a lot like machine guns, too. That's one way to stop people stealing your milk. Neatly packed trays – of, I guessed, bento boxes – were exploding all around me. Pickles, radishes, sushi rolls, things in breadcrumbs, peanuts, bits of mackerel, etc., were raining down. I felt for my purée gun. Naturally, it was gone. It was probably still lying in that giant hollow snail. I looked around for alternative weaponry. On the closest workspace was a sack of sweet potatoes, or some Japanese equivalent.

In history class, Mr Hogstein was always saying I shouldn't slouch and that I had the posture of a sack of potatoes. Hypocrite alert! I remembered this as I ripped open the sack and lobbed some spuds. But

they just sailed through the volley of gunfire and got neatly diced. A slightly too-close-for-comfort *NEOWWWWWW* sound told me that the trench coat had taken a pranging. (As I said earlier, you should always pack a few spares.)

It meant that these robotic machine-gun-toting fridges had some sort of motion-sensor – or they could actually *see* the coat poking out behind the trolley. This gave me an idea. The fridges continued firing. I took off the trench coat. And remembering Hogstein's insult, I used it to wrap up the sack of potatoes. I waited until there was a lull in the fridge-fire and peeped over the parapet. There was a millisecond to act. I flung the trench-coated potato sack into the gap between the two robot fridges.

They spun and fired at the lumpen form between them, thinking it was me, and reduced it to potatoey confetti. But they had caught each other in the crossfire. They weren't the brightest. (I mean, if you hire a pair of fridges to do your dirty work, what do you expect?) Watching them pepper each other, I was mesmerised. First, the bullets just seemed to ricochet and tap dance all over the framework of the fridges. Then they pulverised whatever food was left inside. Then they wiped out the light bulbs and the fans. Which produced some sparks. Which produced some flames. Uh-oh. I'd been here before. I curled into a ball as the explosion unbelted.

After the fiery roar I could hear hunks of wall rumble and collapse, then a powdery fizz as the dust made some attempt at settling. Who'd have thought two dying fridges could sound like World War Three?

I squinted through the miasma. An alarm – better late than never – was screaming its lungs out. A jagged hole smouldered in the wall. Outside lay the edge of a dock and rows of shipping containers, and beyond those, the sea. I stumbled out and over the rubble, past the corpses of the robot fridges, their red lights blinking.

Through the gaps in the shipping containers, the sea beckoned me, an Anchovy to water. But before I could reach it, a tall figure stepped out from behind the last shipping container. A starchy white cloth was draped over one arm. In the other was a harpoon gun. Witherknife smiled, bemused and confused, and fired.

Chapter 13

He should have gone to Specsavers. For a man with glasses that seemed to magnify his eyes by ten, Witherknife's aim wasn't the best. As in the big old house in the countryside, the harpoon missed, whistling into a shipping container instead of impaling me. I shot off to the left, between the containers. I heard butler shoes clicking in the parallel lanes of the container maze, and that fruity voice shout: 'The *other side*, TAFKAR! The *other side*!'

TAFKAR! The Artist Formerly Known As

Rat! I heard footsteps approaching from another direction, lighter and scurrying – appropriately rat-like. My next decision proved to be not exactly fatal, but just gross. It was a risk to run forwards. It was a risk to go back. But each container had a ladder, which maybe led to a hiding place.

The footsteps grew louder. The only way was up. Speed was the chief attribute I was going for. Logic or comfort weren't factored in, so the second I reached the top I flung myself into the container, without checking what lay below.

I landed with a squelch. No one likes a squelch. It's never a nice sound. We associate squelches with boggy dirt, or dirty bogs, and things that are generally nasty and squelchy and going off. But there is a worse sound. It's the sound of flies humming *around* that squelchy thing. That thing, in this case, being an industrial skip full of fish guts. Ironic, really, given my codename.

The fishy punch to the nostrils was so vile that I worried I might never be able to enjoy an anchovy pizza again. I held my breath. Partly so I didn't puke. But also because I could hear one butler and one conceptual artist loitering nearby. A fly began crawling along my nose. It was very ticklish.

'Well, TAFKAR,' I heard Witherknife intone, 'the plot *does* thicken, doesn't it?'

'Haha,' came the ratty one's reply. 'Yes, Mr Witherknife, this is very confusing.'

The fly was apparently a fan of potholing – with my nostril as its cave of choice.

'It's also very annoying, TAFKAR. I'm more annoyed than I am confused. What happened?'

'In Japan, we have an expression – you must never give your mother-in-law unripe eggplants.'

'What on *earth* are you talking about? I want this boy DEAD, do you hear me?!' The fly crawled out and buzzed off. 'Dead! Dead, dead, dead, de– Oh . . . by Jove . . .' I heard a sniffing. 'What happened to the kitchen?'

I looked up from my pit. Black smoke was spilling into the sky.

'The kitchen is on fire, Mr Witherknife. In Japan we say that if you see fire in the kitchen, there must be a raccoon in the cellar –'

'I can *see* that the kitchen is on fire, for crying out loud! How did this happen? You put him in the freezer, didn't you?'

'Yes, Mr Witherknife, the freezer, the one with the fish sticks.'

'This is serious. The boy must be some kind of pyromaniac!'

'Ah, Mr Witherknife, what is this word, a *pie-maniac*?'

Why was everyone calling me that?

'It doesn't matter now . . . Go and put the fire out, TAFKAR!'

'But the boy, Mr Witherknife . . . you say you want him dead, dead, dead?'

'I do, believe me, I do. But that can wait.'

I mentioned squelches being horrible. And the hum of flies being even more horrible. But do you know what's even worse? Maggots. That's right. Maggots. They were wriggling around a nearby fish head, one even looping in and out of the eye sockets like some depraved roller coaster.

'Wait?'

'For the delivery, TAFKAR, for the delivery. It must be made tonight.'

I might well have made a pre-puking *'mfff'* sound. The maggots wriggled closer.

'Ah, I see now. You mean the delivery must be made tonight?'

'Yes, that's what I said. Lord Bobo must be dealt with, don't you understand?' The voices seemed to fade as they edged away. I just about caught the lines, 'Mystery Meats will handle it once it gets to the island . . .'

Mystery Meats! They slunk off and the voices vanished. And did they say *island*? A roll of chunder forced me to hoist myself up and empty my stomach onto the dock below. *Ooof*. I was gathering my strength to climb down the ladder – you know how vomiting takes it out of you – when a mass of blue shadow engulfed me. It was a claw. This claw was attached to a crane. And this crane was attaching itself to my container.

I hoisted myself up onto the ledge. But the blend of fish bits and vom chunks made me slip. Back in I squelched. There was a thunderous **CLANK**. I tried to climb up again, but the container lurched off the ground, teetering in the crane's grip. I scrambled up again, gripping the edge of the now airborne skip. The city helter-skeltered around me: harbour and boats and warehouses and piers smearing into one. I'd seen all this from the plane, in a slightly more serene moment. Figures below me swarmed to put out the fire.

I could also see TAFKAR and Witherknife returning into shot: one short, with red sunglasses and backwards flat cap; the other looming and pristine, built like a fridge himself. They were carrying a creamy-yellow wooden crate – a long one, almost like a coffin. On the side was stencilled the letters: **OCTOBALLS LTD**.

The crane swung me around until I was right above them. I looked into their crate. A great wave of vomit surged in me again. Because stretched out in the crate, deadly pale, with something shiny on his chest, lay the moth-eaten form of Lord Bobo.

No, I muttered to myself. *No, no, no.*

Witherknife and TAFKAR handed Bobo to some guys in overalls. Who then placed a lid over the box and padlocked him in. Then they marched the box up a gangplank, onto a cargo ship, and shoved it into a pile of other crates. It seemed I was joining the club: the crane lowered my container onto the deck.

Now. Now was the time to get out. But where was this cargo ship going? And where was it taking poor Bobo? I slid down the ladder and peeked around the container. To the right was a gaggle of henchmen. And to my left, a second gaggle. How did I know they were henchmen? Because most workers on freight ships don't carry lead pipes, clubs and other thuggish bits of kit. That's a henchman's game.

There was a whack as one of them brought the club down on his open palm and scoured around. He was one of those smokers whose cigarettes stay glued to the mouth even if they're talking.

I heard another **CLANK**. It was another mechanical claw, but more of a mini one, and it had closed its hooks around the railing of the ship. A purple cable was attached to it. And attached to this, poking over the ledge (and hopefully harnessed in), was a blonde head with a wonky fringe.

'Alicia?'

'Col . . .' she gasped. 'What is that *smell*?'

'Fish guts,' I whispered.

'Fish guts? That reminds me, actually . . . I was thinking maybe my codename could be Teeny Sardine-y?'

'Maybe not the best time, Al. We need to save Bobo.'

'Bobo? But we've come here to save you!' She hoisted herself onto the deck.

'We?'

'I'm wiring the guys now. We've been following these sickos but couldn't get into the warehouse. What was it like in there?'

'Cold.'

She typed a message into her watch. 'Loving this pastille watch by the way . . .'

'Great work, Al, great work.' I gave her a high five and she wiped her hand.

'No offence, but you *reek*.'

'Come on,' I sighed. 'Bobo is this way. And from now on, only speak if it's essential – this place is infested with henchmen.'

She made a circle with her forefinger and thumb. We crawled around until we found Bobo's crate. The voices of the hench brigade grew nearer, gossiping on their cigarette break.

BEEP-BEEP.

Alicia was messaging the other G.S.L.-ers.

'Al,' I whispered. 'Put your watch to silent, please. I'll also need to borrow it as mine's down.'

She gave me one of her death stares and handed it over. Even though it was an apprentice version, I remembered it had a laser function. These Japanese models!

'Keep an eye on those guys, will you?' I turned to the fancy padlock and began lasering where the bar joined the main part. 'We need to be really, *really* quiet and not set off any alar–'

NEE-NAW-NEE-NAW-NEE-NAW-NEE-NAW-NEE-NAW-NEE-NAW-NEE-NAW!!

'Looks like you just did,' muttered Alicia. A barrage of boots thundered over the deck. How was I to know it was an electronic padlock?

'Back to your climbing rope,' I said. 'And I'm sorry, Al, but I'll need to take your purée gun.'

Another death stare. She handed it over. The boot thunder grew louder.

'Go!' I shouted, grabbing her hand as we charged back towards the climbing rope. The rope was still in place, but it was being examined by a trio of lead-pipe wielders. We spun around and took another route, up and down a metal staircase, and along another part of the ship. I fired the purée gun, unsuccessfully. Unless you call taking out a window and startling a seagull successful. On we ran. A message flashed up on Alicia's pastille watch: **Get to the front of the ship!**

We heard more tough nuts above us, vaulting over railings.

Added to this challenge of puréeing henchmen and reading messages and sprinting all at the same time were the many ropes, cables, screws and bolts on the deck. Added to this were the metallic projectiles raining down on us. The ship's megaphone crackled to life. I normally associate these with ferry rides to France, where a sleepy captain's voice tells everyone to get in their cars, or that someone's teddy has been found. This ship's loudspeaker had a different message: 'GET THOSE CHILDREN!!!!'

I turned back for a second to see, lurking inside the cabin, a certain butler with a pencil-thin microphone.

'GET THEM!!!!'

We charged onto the prow of the ship. Amid a web of ropes, a nasty-looking artist was toying with a blunt instrument. Alicia's purée gun was out of juice, and just dribbled onto the deck. TAFKAR cackled, rattily. The hench squad loomed closer. TAFKAR advanced and raised his lead pipe. I huddled around Alicia, pressing her into my stomach. Right before I closed my eyes, something black and blurry flashed across the scene.

At first, I thought it was a bird. But then, in surreal slow motion, as I beheld TAFKAR tumble, clutching his face, his sunglasses crumpling, I realised it was the rigging. It had been snapped, whipping him in the kisser. A figure in rainbow-striped socks leapt down from the funnel.

'Norio!' I cried, too astonished to bow. He put a finger to his lips and fired his purée gun towards the advancing henchmen – who, stunned by TAFKAR's collapse, had paused for thought. Norio waved us to the other side of the prow. Over the railing was a rope ladder. Under the rope ladder was a speedboat. In the speedboat was the last person I wanted to owe my freedom to: Pierce Aniseed, looking extra photogenic in a black polo neck and sunglasses, with his blond quiff catching the last shreds of the sunset.

Chapter 14

I guess beggars can't be choosers. We scrambled into the speedboat and scudded out of the harbour. I took the front seat, next to Pierce Aniseed.

'Holy Hovis!' he cried. 'What is that *smell*?!!!'

'Fish guts,' I muttered, blinking back the surf.

'I'll lend you some of my Lynx,' said Pierce Aniseed, rearranging his curls.

I frowned at Alicia, who was making a set of bunny ears behind his head.

'Soooo, guys,' said Pierce Aniseed, 'Princess wants to have a few words with you.'

'Where are we going?!' yelled Alicia.

'You'll see!' said Pierce Aniseed, enjoying the suspense.

I leant back and winced. The lump on my head was still fairly gobstoppery. The pain made the rippling purple-and-yellow sunset seem even more like a giant bruise. I hoped the fresh air would sort out my fish honk.

After a while the speedboat slowed down. I heard Alicia coo so I sat up. We had pulled up at an old steamboat, quietly bobbing in the milky-pink water. A weathered logo of the spatula diamond was painted near the front. Monmon appeared on the railings and threw us a rope with her good hand.

'Sooooo, guys,' purred Pierce Aniseed, catching the rope without even looking. 'We got wind that some suspicious shipments of Octoballs were seen leaving the port.'

'By suspicious shipments,' I offered, 'you mean that crate with an ill-looking Bobo inside.'

Pierce pushed ahead on the steps, thrusting his tank of a backside in my face. 'I don't know about that, Anchovy, but I reckon Lord Bobo is inside those crates. And he might not be looking too fresh right now.'

'But I just said tha—'

'So anyway, that means we'll be transferring operations to the good ship *Saucy Sue* from now on,' lectured Pierce Aniseed. 'I hope you don't get seasick, Anchovy!' He laughed at this non-joke, vaulted onto the deck, and greeted Monmon in his flowing Japanese. 'But first things first: you need a shower ASAP . . . Norio will show you and your apprentice around. Uh, what did you say her name was?'

'I was thinking my codename could be *Cod*zilla,' suggested Alicia.

Aniseed snorted and waved us off. I guessed he had some important toadying to do. I leant against the railings and watched the shrinking, glistening waterfront. A purplish haze hung over the buildings, and beyond them, Mount Fuji, so strangely symmetrical. The last few sunbeams, apricot-red, pulsed like lava on the steamboat's wake. What a day. I'd had high hopes when we'd left the manga fort that morning. Alicia – like a lot of sisters – was a good mind reader.

'Cheer up, Col,' she said, tugging my sleeve, then recoiling at the fish slime. 'You'll feel better after a shower. Which I think we'd all be grateful you had.'

'Yeah,' I mumbled, and we followed Norio into the cabin.

I have to say, after a day of being bludgeoned in a snail sculpture by a conceptual artist, shot at by robot fridges and getting hurled into a pit of fish guts, the steamboat was the perfect place to be. It was like the toy pirate ship I used to play with on the floor of our bedroom, imagining the blue carpet as a limitless ocean. Norio led us through the wood-panelled corridors, first stopping at a narrow room with duck-egg-blue walls, brass-ringed portholes and a dinky kitchen with a long yellow table. 'This blue cabin is our dining area,' said Norio. 'We call it the Blue Dining Cabin. Your dinner will be served here in –' Norio checked his watch '– twenty-eight minutes and forty-two seconds.'

He then led us to another cabin. Inside, Camillo waved from a workbench, before doing some soldering on the turbo-charged pogo stick.

'This is the cabin where we store and make inventions,' said Norio. 'We call it the –'

'Invention Cabin?' ventured Alicia.

'Yes. The Invention Cabin. Here is also stored our mini-sub.'

'A sandwich?'

'No, Al, he means an *actual* mini-sub.'

'Cooooooooool.'

'Yes. I think you know this model, designed by our colleague, Camillo Canteluppi.'

Norio led us out and further along the corridor.

'This is the cabin for special guests. We call it the Special Guest Cabin.'

Something white and slinky jumped off the bunkbed and purred against Alicia's leg.

'Bernard!'

Norio smiled bashfully. I had the sneaking suspicion Bernard had been smuggled in against the express orders of Princess Skewer. Norio showed us the bathroom, towels, slippers, changes of clothes and the button to press if we needed anything, then bowed and left. A sweet kid. Why couldn't I have an apprentice like that?

After I'd had the world's longest shower and

Alicia had some quality Bernard-time, we headed to the imaginatively named Blue Dining Cabin. Monmon was there, too, and Norio had some huge pot sizzling. He served us tofu and broth and seaweed in a beautiful ceramic box.

After that, on a full belly, we could finally do some detective work.

'So,' Monmon said, 'let's talk about what we know so far. Norio-kun?'

Norio took out a pen and a notebook wrapped in marbled paper.

'Bobo is in a packing crate,' I began, starting with the most urgent thing.

'We know that Witherknife is organising this,' said Monmon.

'And so is that weirdo artist,' added Alicia.

'Ah, you mean TAFKAR,' said Monmon grimly, as Norio jotted it all down.

'But no sign of Mystery Meats since that raid

on the Good Luck Fishcake,' I said. 'Although apparently he's going to deal with the crates on some island.'

'Which island?' said Alicia.

'We're tracking the capercorder,' said Monmon. 'It is going to an island called Kirajima. We will go there tomorrow to investigate. Perhaps we will learn more about Mystery Meats.'

'And hopefully get Bobo . . .' I muttered, even though I was fearing the worst.

'What kind of creepazoid calls themselves Mystery Meats?' said Alicia.

'Working hard?' broke in a sarcastic voice. Pierce Aniseed had stuck his head in, peering over us like some human action figure. He leant over Monmon's notebook, raised his eyebrows, then ducked out again.

We helped wash up. Norio, who was such a perfectionist washer-upper, explained that in

Japanese schools there is a session every week for kids to clean or scrub something – and to learn how to clean properly. He'd be horrified at Caesar Pizza. Alicia and I never got *all* the sweetcorn out of our big dishwasher.

Us Kingsleys were exhausted by nine and, thanking Norio for the tasty meal, we padded to our cabin to get some well-earnt sleep. The lump on my head was still ringing. What a life!

Down the corridor, light shone from a cabin I hadn't seen before. Inside, the voice of Pierce Aniseed was protesting about something. I tiptoed closer to eavesdrop. Nosy of me, I know, but show me a detective who says they aren't nosy and I'll show you a liar.

'Princess,' he began, 'please, Princess, with your wise and wonderful leadership skills –' (yuck!) '– you, Princess Skewer, know better than anyone that the personnel on this case is simply not good enough!'

I couldn't see Princess, but I guessed by the pause that she had her poker face on.

'What are you implying, Pierce?'

'What I'm implying, or rather, wise and wonderful Princess, *recommending*, is that we find a replacement for Detective Anchovy. Immediately.'

I felt the tofu tumble-dry in my belly. *Replace* me?

'Just a *thought*, Princess, of course,' Pierce squirmed on, 'and as we all know, you're the boss –'

'That's a little drastic, Pierce, and I'm not sure I understand what you're driving at.'

'Allow me to explain, Princess.'

'Gladly.'

'I've made a Catalogue of Misdemeanours for the detective in question. I can read it out.'

What?! I thought that was only for apprentices!

'If you must.'

'Ahem. Catalogue of Misdemeanours for the Caterer Detective Mark Anchovy, compiled by Pierce Aniseed, Personal Assistant to Branch Preside–'

'Just give me the list, Pierce.'

'Very well. Item One: Allowed apprentice to stowaway on an unrelated case. Item Two: Allowed apprentice to eat an important alibi. Item Three: Allowed apprentice to almost drown history teacher.'

Ex-history teacher, but whatever.

'Item Four: Altercation with prime suspect in a country mansion with a failure to arrest and detain the aforementioned.'

He had a harpoon gun!

'Item Five: Failure to prevent prime suspect assaulting Japanese colleague, Detective Monmon Miguomo.'

I still felt bad about that.

'Item Six: Ongoing failure to distribute G.S.L. tattoo to apprentice.'

Come on . . . really?

'Item Seven: Shot a caper at me, which got stuck in my newly washed hair.'

I mean, this guy was just taking the absolute biscuit now. Plus, that was Alicia.

'Item Eight: Allowed himself to be captured by a conceptual artist . . .' He paused to snigger, before continuing. 'Item Nine: Set a kitchen on fire – which, looking through past records, is the third – no, *fourth* such recorded incident of this type during his employment with us, implying that this detective may be some sort of pyromaniac.'

This was beyond ridiculous. I barely ever ate pies!

'Item Ten: Set off an alarm on a freight ship, failing to secure the rescue of Lord Bobo, whom we've been employed to protect and return to safety.'

Anything else?

'Oh, and Item Eleven: Refused the offer of my Lynx deodorant.'

'Okay, Pierce,' cut in Princess, mercifully. 'I get the picture. I appreciate that Mark Anchovy is, how can I put it . . . ? A little erratic.'

'A little?!' gasped Pierce Aniseed.

'I know Anchovy well,' said Princess. 'He fluffs up the basics, yes, and generally takes a pretty roundabout way to get the job done.'

'My point exactly,' said Pierce Aniseed.

'*But,*' stressed Princess, reaching into her bag of conversational clubs for something more heavy duty, 'he *does* get the job done, and he *has* pulled off some pretty unlikely triumphs in his time.' I gave a fist-pump in the corridor. *In your handsome face, Aniseed.* Princess went on.

'There are only a handful of photographic-memory guys working these days, and for someone still starting out, he's up there with the best. We certainly will *not* be replacing him. And for the record, who uses Lynx? It smells like cough medicine mixed with cat urine!'

'But Princess . . . just think how much these catastrophes are costing us!'

'Perhaps you didn't hear me correctly, Pierce. Listen, you've been a fantastic PA – always so useful to have someone who speaks perfect Japanese – but you're being *bang* out of order. Anchovy stays!'

I think I may have done a little hula dance.

'Of course, Princess, of course,' panted Pierce Aniseed. I noticed he'd dropped the 'wise and wonderful' slush. 'As you wish.'

I couldn't see him – either of them – but I could see Pierce's shadow on the cabin wall, his perfect profile magnified and silhouetted. And as I looked closely, a cold sweat broke over me. That silhouette . . . the chiselled nose . . . the mop of curly quiff . . . the figure in the alley jumping through the van's sunroof . . . it was uncanny:

Mystery Meats was among us!

Chapter 15

'm always astonished that G.S.L. travel kits don't contain a whack of sleeping pills. We catering detectives need them. While Alicia snored like an orchestra of pneumatic drills, I lay awake, staring at the ceiling. I thought about what I'd seen in Princess's office. Was it merely a trick of the light? Was my brain just wired from too many dances with danger? But if it wasn't, how could I warn Princess without Pierce 'Mystery Meats' Aniseed cutting me off in my prime?

My jumpy brain finally packed in, but only for a few hours. I was woken by an almighty

HONNNNNNKKKKKKKK!

Searching for the source, I scowled at Alicia's bunk. But she was up and out. The pizza watch said 8:30 a.m. Outside the porthole came another *HONNNKKK,* this time accompanied by a chorus of seagulls and the sea sliding by, grey-blue with firecracker shards of morning sun.

'Lazy bones ahoy!!' shouted Alicia, strolling in with two fluffy white buns wrapped in spiky pink paper, with yellow bits of fruit on top – possibly pineapple. She passed me one.

'Thanks, Al.'

'It's actually not bad. Sort of like candy floss.'

Candy floss for breakfast? Why not. It went down pretty easily, the pineapple's tang stirring me to life. After I'd licked my fingers, I cupped a hand over my mouth.

'Al – word to the wise,' I whispered. 'Stay away from Pierce Aniseed.'

'Way ahead of you, bro. I've been giving him the cold shoulder since we got here.'

'Just don't talk to him, okay? He could be dangerous.'

'Yeah. That deodorant makes me almost pass out. What is it? Floor polish mixed with dog vom or something?'

'It's more serious than that. He's –'

There was a cough at the door. I spun around, all of a jitter, the fluffy bun now doing a tango with yesterday's tofu. But it was only Monmon.

'*Ohayo gozaimasu,*' she said with a bow. 'There is a meeting in the Invention Cabin in ten minutes.' A super-speedy shower, a fresh trench coat and I was ready.

The rest of the team was already seated around the workstation in the laboratory. Camillo was pumping up a balloon version of a cat shaped like a bus. Pierce Aniseed was sulkily yanking the projector screen. He saw me and glared. Norio distributed little teapots and green-glazed ceramic beakers. Princess was at the head, her fingers laced together. I smiled at her and she nodded back with a half-smile, which became a non-smile when she saw Bernard tucked under Alicia's arm.

'Who allowed that flea-ridden stray cat to come on board?'

'Some tea, Princess Skewer-san,' interrupted Norio wisely, and poured out a beaker. He bowed and left.

'*Arigato*,' said Princess. 'I suppose we should get started. So, team, we're approaching the island of Kirajima.' A map of the island came up on the screen. I noticed Pierce Aniseed frantically taking notes. When was I going to get a moment alone with Princess to warn her?! Princess continued. 'We know that Bobo is being held captive on Kirajima – probably somewhere hidden and secret.

Anchovy, what was his condition when you saw him last?'

I bit my lip.

'Not great.'

'"Not great" as in still-twitching-with-signs-of-life, or the *other* "not great"?'

'Hard to tell,' I said optimistically, picturing the pallid Bobo in the crate. 'But hold on . . .' I was getting another detail as I froze the film still of that moment in my camera-brain. There had been something shiny on his chest. I zoomed in on it. It was a small plastic square on a cord around his neck. It looked like an ID or security pass.

'What is it, Anchovy?' asked Princess.

I closed my eyes, trying to focus, going into my memory-trance.

'He does this sometimes,' I heard Alicia tell the others.

My camera-brain zoomed in again. On the

plastic card was a mugshot of Lord Bobo, with his name printed below as 'Mr Bobo'. Above it were smaller letters, in both Japanese and in English. I zoomed in again and read aloud what I saw:

Lionpaw Towers, English School.

'Good work, Anchovy,' said Princess. (Pierce Aniseed winced.) 'Monmon – what do we know about Kirajima? Is there an English school there?'

Monmon took the floor.

'Kirajima is a very small island. It does not have many things there. There are some famous art sculptures and galleries . . . there is also a village with a temple. And also some shops and houses. Some factories that make things with copper, also. And a school, yes.'

'An English school?'

'Yes. It is a very famous but also very secret place for children who have lots of money.'

Camillo then grabbed his weird helium

cat balloon – which was apparently remote controlled – and began untying something from the end of it. 'Actually,' he said, 'earlier we made photographs of the island using this special camera. There is the school on here.' He pointed to the map. 'Up on the, ah . . . *cliffs*.'

'Thanks, Cam,' said Princess. 'Anchovy, and . . . erm . . . what are you calling yourself today?' She at least gave Alicia a smile and a wink.

'I was thinking my codename could be Cray-Cray Fish?'

'Niche,' said Princess. 'Anyway, follow me. No, Pierce – you stay here.'

She led us up on deck, where Norio was perched like a figurehead, gazing through a telescope. It was a glorious day, with the craggy haunch of Kirajima looming above us, its cliff face dotted with moss and little birds bawling like gossipy neighbours. On the clifftop lay a cluster of white school buildings, with a steep track winding to a beach below.

'Princess,' said Monmon, 'I think we should maybe pack for "Surveillance By Sea: Intermediate Level 4". Is that okay?'

Princess nodded thoughtfully as she looked through Norio's telescope. 'Yep. Do we have enough wetsuits?'

'*Wetsuits?*' said Alicia, aghast.

'Shish kebab!!' Princess was training the telescope on Lionpaw Towers. An ant-like procession of black-and-white dots was spilling from the school. 'You're not going to believe this,' said Princess, and handed me the telescope.

The dots, magnified with impressive power, were schoolchildren in crisp white shirts, black blazers, matching bucket-y hats and (I think) jelly shoes. They trickled down in a crocodile formation, carrying rucksacks, clipboards, water bottles and fishing nets. At one point they saw our ship and waved. They headed to the beach. There was a teacher at the back, mouthing a quick headcount. I scanned to the front and almost dropped the telescope in shock. Nimbly leading the way, in a black suit and tie and a bowler hat, with his moustache a little less droopy, his face a lot less pallid, was the students' other teacher. Or, as we knew him, Lord Bobo.

Chapter 16

Pierce Aniseed's face was framed in a grimy porthole, caught between a squint and a scowl. It was my last impression of the ship as we dived into the waters, all scuba-geared up. The bubbles roared around us, rupturing the silence of the turquoise world below. I didn't want to think too much about what was scuttling and wriggling down there. Alicia was a strong swimmer – maybe because she's an Aquarius – and zoomed ahead of Norio and I, her flippers motoring up the foam.

To stay hidden, we approached via a rocky

archway to the side of the beach. With underwater hand signals, Norio motioned for us to be careful of all the sea urchins, lurking blood-red on the green-gold rocks. We bobbed up under a ledge, removing our mouthpieces with a plunger-like smack, and scanned the beach. The ant procession of children filed into view. Bobo and the other teacher did an extra headcount.

'Col— I mean, Anchovy,' gargled Alicia, after spitting out a mouthful of saltwater. 'Can I pee in the sea here?'

'Not this particular bit of sea while I'm in it. Can't you hold it in?'

She shook her head. Her stubborn frown was then replaced by a dreamy look of relief, which was followed by a smirk.

'ALIIIIIIIIIIIICIA KINGSLEYYYYYYYY!!!!!!!!'

'What is happening, please?' said Norio.

I thought it was better not to tell him. I made

a mental note for the Catalogue of Apprentice Misdemeanours and Offences: *Peed on me.*

At this moment, curse him, Bobo decided to lead his troops over our rocky ledge, and as luck would *not* have it, we had to duck down into the now slightly warmer water. We bobbed up again after the footfall had passed. I was seriously considering applying to have my apprentice exchanged.

Bobo and his co-teacher were escorting the kids over an outcrop jutting out into the sea, swooshing their nets in and out of the rockpools. Bobo, a teacher. I didn't get it. I thought I'd seen this man lying prone in a packing crate. And that three vicious assassins were after him. Why? I know we can all have *some* beef with our teachers – but chasing him around the world with a harpoon gun? Even if he had sentenced them to a *lifetime* of detentions, it seemed extreme.

I have to say, Bobo seemed pretty used to this teaching lark. He was telling everyone to be careful on the rocks and tried to explain long, waffly concepts like coastal erosion and something else I missed. Bobo then wandered to the centre of the outcrop to inspect a crab that was picking away at some bumpy yellow seaweed. He then spun around as something splashed. I had hoped it would be a dolphin, or a seal, or some kid throwing a large rock in the sea just for the hell of it. But it wasn't. It was a figure, emerging from the water in tight black shorts, a snorkel in one hand and a purée gun in the other, *sprinting towards Bobo*. Yes, it was Pierce Aniseed.

'Stop right there!' he was screaming. 'Stop!!'

The schoolkids gawped in unison at this terrifying weirdo, then huddled around the other teacher.

Now wasn't the time for analysing. I vaulted

onto the ledge and hurtled towards him.

'It's Mystery Meeeeeeeeeats!!' I yelled to Bobo. 'Get down!!'

My irritation at Pierce Aniseed gave me extra speed, but there was one small problem. Have you ever tried sprinting in flippers? Don't. There was a crescendo of slaps and before I knew it I was toppling to the ground. The nearest thing to cushion my fall was . . . well, Pierce Aniseed. This accidental rugby tackle also sent Pierce toppling.

'Noooooooo!' he screamed. 'Get off me, Anchovy! Get off me, you idiot! You're ruining everything!! Nooooo!' And he then started babbling in fluent Japanese. Which was just showing off. We tussled on the knobbly rockface, sharp points and limpet shells pranging us in the fleshy parts.

'Fight! Fight! Fight!' I heard Alicia bawl, clapping her little hands. A detective possessed,

I managed to grapple Pierce Aniseed's purée
gun out of his hand. But the guy was built like a
brick shish-kebab house and his thunder thighs
pummelled me off.

'Stop, Anchovy!' he screamed. If witnessing two
random Brits wrestling in front of them (one in a
wetsuit, the other semi-naked) wasn't confusing
enough for Lord Bobo and the schoolkids, what
happened next bamboozled them beyond belief. A
mini-earthquake struck. Well, it felt like a mini-
earthquake. The outcrop began to rumble, and
as I looked, a crack started tracing a perfect circle
around Bobo. A hole opened up and, in the blink
of an eye, Lord Bobo vanished into oblivion.

The shock of this gave Pierce Aniseed a chance
to boot me off him once more. Norio rushed onto
the scene and separated us. I think I may have even
growled. We staggered to the edge of the hole, but
all we could see was the deepest, darkest void I

could ever have imagined.

'Anchovy,' panted Pierce Aniseed, 'you *idiot*! It's Witherknife's trap! This was what I was trying to warn him about! Now we've lost Lord Bobo!!'

There was a long, painful pause.

'Oops,' said Alicia.

Chapter 17

The worst part of Princess Skewer's reaction – the part that really cut me down – was that she didn't even get angry. She laced her hands, the index fingers forming a steeple, and then kneaded the bridge of her nose, before heaving a long, tremoring sigh. Somehow, her disappointment felt worse than anger. At the opposite end of the office sat Pierce Aniseed, bandaged and bruised. Norio stood in the centre. Monmon watched from afar. I sat with Alicia, who was stroking Bernard in an agitated manner. Princess addressed Norio.

'So, one last time,' she asked. 'As a witness, you can confirm that Pierce's allegations are true. Anchovy attacked him on the rocks . . .' Norio wasn't a dobber. But he couldn't lie here; I'll hold up my hand – I did sort of attack Pierce Aniseed. Norio nodded. Princess stared intently. 'And you confirm, also, that this directly led to the sudden disappearance of Lord Bobo.' Norio was more reluctant with the second nod, but it was a nod all the same. 'I see. Please take a seat.'

Norio went and slumped on a bench. Princess mused, gazing at the ceiling.

'Power. Power is a curious thing, you know.' It felt like she'd rehearsed these lines. 'Because with great power, Anchovy, comes GIGANTIC responsibility.'

'I think it's just *great* responsibility, Princess,' interjected P̲ratty A̲ssistant.

'Enough, Pierce.' She brought out some salmon-pink papers with a red banner across them. I didn't like the look of this. 'Bring me the full charge sheet as well, please.' Pierce Aniseed stood up and, from a filing cabinet, passed Princess a thin sheet of paper with writing on it in a light-blue table. As he sat down, his left eyeball seemed to spasm with triumph. Princess read the charge sheet and stamped the top-right corner.

'Stand up, you two.'

In my past cases, I'd got away with some pretty hefty tickings-off from the G.S.L. But an inner voice whispered that my luck had run out. Princess straightened the papers and read in a solemn, robotic voice.

'Caterer Detective Mark Anchovy, it is my painful duty to inform you and your apprentice that your employment with the Golden Spatula League is hereby officially terminated.'

My world collapsed.

'What does "terminated" mean?' whispered Alicia, tugging my sleeve.

'This decision,' continued Princess, rubbing her eyes, 'is one which I am compelled to make in light of both a growing list of misdemeanours and, specifically, your actions today. While we are aware of the contributions you have made to the agency over the past year, we cannot sanction an assault on another member of staff. You are dismissed with *immediate effect*. Arrangements have already been made for your return to Rufflington-on-Sea tomorrow morning. All G.S.L. possessions and equipment must be deposited in the box in the corner, including your watches, purée guns, superglue cufflinks, iron-shoes and any other sundries accrued during your employment. You may take your, er, civilian clothes – oh, and that double-bass case.'

'Now?' I asked, in a voice that sounded much

mousier than I ever imagined it could.

'Now.'

We emptied our pockets, our gadgets landing in the box with a horrible clang. Pierce Aniseed peered at this with special interest.

'Where's your watch, apprentice?' he quizzed Alicia. 'That also needs to go in there.'

'Sorry, personal assistant,' replied Alicia, 'but it fell off in the sea.'

'Fell off in the sea? Yeah, right!' snorted Pierce. 'Monmon, search her!'

Princess sighed and kneaded her temples as Monmon reluctantly frisked Alicia for the pastille watch. She even ran a special scanner over her, like you do in airports. Harsh. What was one pastille watch to them?

'Nothing here,' said Monmon.

Alicia did a little shoulder-brush at Pierce and slung on her double-bass case. Bernard hissed.

Princess read on. 'Please be informed that on your return to Rufflington, you will find that your secret office beneath Caesar Pizza has been removed and is no longer accessible. A laser surgeon has also been booked to remove your G.S.L. tattoo.'

Alicia hadn't even got a G.S.L. tattoo yet . . . perhaps that was a good thing. Laser surgery!

'As you are well aware,' continued Princess, 'employment with the Golden Spatula League is a matter of the utmost confidentiality, for both current and former detectives. You are contractually obliged to maintain secrecy regarding your employment with us, even in the event of dismissal. Failure to do so will incur strong repercussions, as stated in your contract on page 47, clause 4d.'

It was like my entire G.S.L. career had never happened.

'It only remains for me to say how extremely disappointed I am to see your time with the G.S.L. end in this fashion, Anchovy.' For the first time during the entire reading, she looked me in the eyes. 'We all had such hopes for you.'

Ouch. Ouch, ouch, ouch.

I had nothing to say. Even Alicia was silent. Princess turned to Norio. At least his rainbow-striped socks provided something cheerful to look at.

'Norio-kun, please escort Anchovy and his apprentice to the Isolation Cabin. And take that mangy alley cat while you are at it.'

Norio mostly concealed his disbelief, but you could still detect a little eyebrow jiggle. I'm not sure how we even got out of the office, staggering as if in quicksand. I didn't want to offend the eyeballs by looking at Pierce Aniseed, but I looked at Princess one last time. The documents screened her – only the ponytail on top of her head was visible, arcing above the pink papers.

'Goodbye, Princess.'

'Goodbye.'

Norio led us along corridors, right to the other end of the ship. 'This is the cabin we use for isolation,' he said in a quiet voice. 'We call it –'

'The Isolation Cabin, yeah, we get it,' interrupted Alicia, still moody from the watch search. 'Isolation Cabin' was actually quite generous. Why not just the Prison Cell Cabin? Because with its stone-hard bunks and barred porthole, that was what it was. And the fact that when Norio shut the heavy-duty door, he locked it. It was this – the clicking sound of doom – that made me snap into life.

'Norio!' I shouted. 'What are you doing? Come on!'

I didn't hear him move away.

'Come on, Norio!' I shouted again. 'I know you're there! You can't lock us in like this!'

Alicia put down Bernard and started pounding on the door.

'Come on, Norio!' she bawled. 'You'd rugby tackle Pierce Aniseed, too, if you had the chance!'

Norio coughed. I mean, it was something. He wasn't disagreeing. It gave me a teeny sliver of hope.

'I am sorry about your situation,' he said in a soft voice.

'Come on, Norio,' I repeated. 'You understand it, don't you? Aniseed did all this to set us up! He's plotting against us! Against all of us! You need to warn Princess . . .'

'And you need to let us out of here!' said Alicia. 'This is what Aniseed wants!'

'Norio,' I continued, 'if we can get out of here, go to the island and find Bobo, prove Aniseed's guilt, then maybe everything will be okay!'

'Hmmm . . .' said Norio. I could almost hear the cogs turning in his brain.

'I know you can see it, Norio,' I continued, surprised by my powers of persuasion. 'You're a good judge of character. You can see all of Aniseed's lies. All his plans for power. He has been trying to get me fired for a long time!'

'I see,' Norio coughed again. 'I see that there is some troubles with Pierce Aniseed-san. Also, what is the deodorant he is using? It is like cheap plum wine combined with fox faeces.'

'Yes!' said Alicia. 'That's so it!'

'Let's stick to the point,' I said, although in theory I agreed. 'Norio, can you help us?'

'Go on, Norio,' cooed Alicia, backing me up. 'All you've got to do is just drop that little key of yours, absent-mindedly, close enough to the crack of the door, and walk off. Just a simple mistake, that's all. No one will fire you for it!'

Norio paused.

'Or,' said Alicia, 'if you want it to be more realistic, we could tie you up and slap you around a bit?'

'No,' said Norio, and he walked off.

'Well done, Al,' I snapped. 'You had to talk about roughing him up, didn't you?'

'Just trying to help, Col, sheesh!' Her lip began to wobble. At least I'd had a few missions with the G.S.L. Alicia's career was over before it had even started. Tears began trickling down her cheeks. I put my arm around her and ruffled her hair.

'I'm sorry, Al. Come on – we'll work something out, won't we?' She nodded and I wiped her cheeks.

'Can Bernard come with us?'

'Of course,' I said. I'd grown attached to Bernard. The accusation that he had fleas or mange was just, well, pure slander.

'What were you even planning? I mean, once we get out of this stupid Isolation Cabin?'

In all honesty, I hadn't come up with a plan A. Or a plan B. Or a plan C. Not that I told Alicia this.

As you can imagine, time weighs pretty heavily inside an Isolation Cabin. Nothing to do except watch your apprentice do chin-ups on the bunk bed and stare out of the porthole as the daylight fades. I can't even pretend the sea view was calming – no moon, no stars, just a slurping black mass with the odd dribble of foam. It may as well have been tarmac. I cranked up my brain power to formulate a possible plan. But the brain cogs were struggling. It might have been Bernard's mewling or Alicia's chin-ups that put me off. Or the general hopelessness of the situation. The brain cogs gave up. Sleep, that old party-pooper, slugged me out at last.

Chapter 18

It was a beautiful sound that stirred us, tinkling like rain on a parched summer garden. Then came the swish of footsteps, flitting from the door. I bent down to look under the crack. Glistening in the dust lay a silver key. Alicia read my mind and passed me a hairpin.

'*Yes*, Norio,' she whispered.

We unbent the hairpin – it was rookie of Pierce Aniseed to miss that – and coaxed in the key. Alicia held it up, like a pearl dredged from the seabed.

'What now, Col?'

Beyond the bars, a lead-blue dawn crept over the waves. The cogs were finally turning.

'The mini-sub,' I whispered.

While I wasn't so into prison movies that I needed to do chin-ups in my cellmate's face, I did know this: when planning an escape, know the layout.

Before unlocking the door then, we took a shoe, a cap and an almost-finished packet of Fruit Pastilles, and positioned them to represent the layout of the ship. If the Isolation Cabin (represented by the stump of the Fruit Pastilles packet) was here and, accordingly, the office of Princess and her Pathetic Assistant was here (represented by the cap), then in theory the Invention Cabin containing the mini-sub was here (represented by the shoe). There was a fair old distance between all three.

This meant that a) we'd probably run into

someone and b) that someone might not be as nice as Norio and could possibly reek of Lynx and c) if this happened, we'd need a plan. We argued over this plan, tweaked it, argued a bit more, tweaked it again, ate the remaining Fruit Pastilles – Alicia gave the last one to Bernard, which was a waste – and agreed that like any plan it might work, or it might be a total flop. There was only one way to find out.

With our shoes off, we padded around the corner, along the landing of the lower deck, and passed Princess's office. Thankfully the light was off. So far so good – as long as Bernard didn't mewl his mouth off. Bernard, bless him, didn't mewl – his mouth wasn't the problem. It was his other end. As we entered the final corridor, the unmistakable sound of a cat-parp filled the air.

'Holy pepperoni!' I gagged, fanning the air. 'Alicia! Why did you give him a Fruit Pastille!'

On cue, as if to demonstrate my point, Bernard parped again.

'How was I supposed to know that gelatine makes him gassy?' protested Alicia.

Bernard – clearly one of those rare breeds that specialise in both volume *and* odour – added a third parp. The pastille (a green one, as I remember) was playing havoc with his innards. He added a fourth, extra-generous parp. At this, a light went on in one of the cabins on the corridor. I grabbed Bernard and hurried us along, hoping I'd get past the door before the occupant opened it. I didn't. Stepping out with a strawberry-red face, a towel around his neck, jogging pants on and some sort of smoothie in his hand was everybody's favourite PA. Fresh from some early-morning workout like the whack job he was. Bernard, jolted by the shock, added a fifth parp.

'What are you DOING?!' Aniseed screamed

and towered above me, dashing his smoothie to the floor. He rolled up his sleeves, Popeye-style. I know that we were two versus one. But that doesn't mean much when that 'one' happens to be a human tank.

'You sneaky little RAT, Anchovy! Sneaking out of your Isolation Cabin! What are you trying to do, huh? Sneaking around the ship like a little sneak-mouse, huh?!'

He did seem overly fond of the word 'sneak'. He grabbed me by the scruff of the trench coat. I didn't have my purée gun any more. I didn't have my superglue cufflinks. But I did have a flatulent cat. It was one of those flashes of inspiration that it's best not to overthink. Spinning Bernard around – bottom forward, if you get me – I lifted his tail, gave his tummy a good squeeze and, right in Pierce Aniseed's face, allowed Bernard to unleash hell. Pleasingly, our feline friend had saved the best until last.

The sixth parp could only be described as a
sort of death-trumpet, producing a grimace of
confusion, queasiness and maybe even delirium
in Aniseed's finely chiselled features. His eyelids
drooped, the colour drained out of his face and,
releasing his clutch on my coat, he tottered back,
slipped on the smoothie and crashed into his cabin.
Bernard added a seventh parp for good measure,

but it was unnecessary. Aniseed was out for the count.

'That's m'boy!' Alicia yelled. She scooped him up and we legged it to the Invention Cabin. From the glow of a monitor, showing a moustachioed pig riding a red plane, we could make out the layout of Camillo's laboratory. The steps leading to the hatch of the mini-sub were at the back. This was good. The lock on the hatch less so. Lockpicking had never been my bag – something I'd usually watch as Master Key or Camillo or Princess did the honours. But now they were gone from my life. Alicia was looking pretty casual, all things considered.

'Any ideas, Al?'

'I thought you might try lasering it, no?'

'What, and set off another alarm?'

'Or we can just wait here for Piddle Aniseed to wake up for round two.'

'Okay, okay, I get that we have to do something. But laser it with what?'

'Have you noticed anything different about Bernard this morning?'

'Don't change the subject to Bernard's bowel movements.'

'I'm not! Take a look at him.' I peered at the cat in question. 'See anything?'

'A new collar. And?'

'Sloppy, Col, sloppy. Look again.'

She held Bernard closer. Thankfully head first. I got it. It wasn't a collar at all: around his neck Bernard was sporting Alicia's pastille watch, with its handy laser feature. I smiled and prised it off.

'Good work, Al. Probably best step back.' I got lasering. Sparks flew up from the lock. 'You know,' I said, 'unfortunately we can't take this with us – they'll be able to track us with it.'

She hung her head and jutted out her lip,

then began fidgeting with the tools on Camillo's workbench. The lock made a faint pop and the hatch loosened. I hoisted it up, stuck my feet through and yanked Alicia in after me. 'Come on, you'll like this.'

I hadn't been in the mini-sub since my first mission in Rome, when Princess, who was then my mentor, had driven it through the sewers. I was hoping I could remember enough of that occasion and my super-crammed training manual. As we settled in, there was a crash in the laboratory. I pressed what I hoped would be the ignition button and heard the bubbles roar. A turbine whirred. Lights beamed on. I grabbed a lever and lucked out.

Off we bubbled. A purple dot pulsed on the monitor, ploughing a course for the green blob of Kirajima. I managed to breathe again. Okay, so I could drive this thing. If my luck held out, I might be able to park it.

'Ewwww, gross,' moaned Alicia, her nose against the porthole glass. Something slimy swam past.

'Don't think about it,' I said, trying and failing to sound casual. 'Whatever's out there is probably more scared of us than we are of it.'

'Well, it's okay, I've got this.' And she opened up the double-bass case. I gazed at the loot inside, horrified. She'd ransacked the Invention Cabin while I was working the lock.

'Did you really need to steal that —' I read the label '— Bubble-tea Bazooka?'

'I prefer the term "borrow" actually.' She resumed her nose-press against the glass. 'Colin . . . are we, like, expelled now?'

'Yes.'

'Expelled expelled, or just suspended for a bit? You know, like Dexter was when he put your head in the —'

'Expelled as in we can't come back, Al,' I said.

'But I'm hoping that if we find Bobo, they might rethink their decision.'

'And realise that Pierce Aniseed is a dirty worm!'

'Yes, that too.'

She rubbed Bernard behind his ear.

'But . . . Colin . . . what if they don't believe us?'

'Well . . .' I peered ahead, into the deep, dark blue. 'Erm . . .'

She turned to me, her eyes widening. 'I really wanted to be a detective . . .'

Our floodlight illuminated a bank of barnacles, rising like an army of waving hands. I half thought I saw a seahorse, jerkily dancing as if on a string.

'Maybe,' I said with a smile, 'we can form our own detective agency.'

'Will it have gadgets?'

'Erm . . . I'll need to see . . .'

'Will it have a private plane?'

'Perhaps not right away.'

'Or a mini-sub?'

'It's hard to park them at Rufflington, to be honest, Al. But we can make a new secret office . . .'

'With a fake revolving door that operates with a mechanical switch disguised as a dented tomato can?'

'We could try something similar, I guess.'

'And would I have a cool codename?'

'Of course, that would be no problem.'

'And we could make some new business cards with our codenames on?'

'Easy peasy.'

'I was thinking maybe I could be called Lady Laserbeam.'

'Maybe, yes, maybe . . .'

'And maybe Bernard could be called the Gassy Assassin. Or just Gasassin.'

'Well, we'd need to see what names are already taken in the detective world, but sure.'

She clapped her hands, which startled Bernard a bit. Thankfully he wasn't living up to his proposed codename in this very small, airtight space. The seabed gradually rose, a hazy, mould-green mosaic, with little fish darting from sandy clumps and long-snouted, white-whiskered fish snaffling around. The purple dot grew, closing in on Kirajima. I hit the buttons I thought Princess had pressed when we had surfaced in Rome.

'Have a look through the periscope, Al,' I said, 'and help me with the jetty.'

'Okay, you're fine,' she said. 'All good, all good, keep going, keep going, keep going, keep –'

There was a bassy **BOOM** as we collided with something stony.

'Okay, stop.'

'Ten seconds earlier would've been nice, but fine,' I muttered, fumbling for the brakes. 'Hit the hatch.'

We clambered onto the jetty via a seaweed-stained ladder. A few peachy sun streaks lit up the harbour. Fishing boats bobbed, nodding as if stirring from a dreamless sleep. Calm. Quiet. At least for a few seconds. A familiar **beeeeeeeeeeeeeeeeeep** disturbed the peace. I glared at my apprentice.

'That had *better* not be a pastille watch.' She hadn't got her lying face ready. 'Alicia Kingsley!' I shouted. 'I told you to get rid of that! Hand it over!'

Huffing and snuffling, she brought out the offending object. I snatched it and lifted the watch face. Text flashed on the screen.

ESCAPE DETECTED, ESCAPE DETECTED . . . then: **LOCATION DETECTED, LOCATION DETECTED** . . . then: **YOU'LL PAY FOR THIS, ANCHOVY. YOU'LL PAY FOR THIS, YOU SNEAK-MOUSE. P.A.**

P.A. – the sight of those initials made up my

mind for me. I went to the end of the jetty and
flung the watch into the sea.

'Urghhhhhhh!' gasped Alicia.

'From now on,' I said, 'when I tell you to throw
away a device that's tracking our movements and
getting us into trouble, you throw it away, okay?'

'But it was a *pastille watch*!'

'I don't care if it's a gold-plated Rolex. People
are after us!'

I picked up the double-bass case. 'Come on.'

We headed towards what looked like the main village.

'Col . . .'

'What do you want now?'

'Breakfast?'

I sighed, and as if by some mechanical effect, my stomach sighed, too.

'Sure.'

Chapter 19

The alleys, with their watering cans, hanging baskets and the occasional racoon statue, looked as dead to the world as we were. Alarmingly, posters were splattered on sliding doors, telegraph poles and trees, bearing the face of 'Mr Bobo'. There were red letters, which probably said 'MISSING', and numbers, which probably meant reward money. He was a popular teacher. I couldn't imagine what we'd raise if Mr Hogstein had gone missing. A few quid?

Knowing that Pierce Aniseed was on our tail,

every street corner gave me the jitters. Equally scary was the noise of my stomach. Earthquake-esque. In the end, our noses led us.

Through a gap in the wooden houses, something sweet and buttery wafted our way. A shutter had opened in a booth by a crossroads. Inside, a man with a broken nose whisked a vat of batter. As we approached, he poured the batter into waffle moulds shaped like little fish. Was it a sign? An omen? I smiled at the man. He didn't smile back.

I took off my shoe and sock, and, somewhat off balance, showed him Markus Anchovius. A finger tattoo would've been much better. The waffle man looked baffled. He wasn't G.S.L. Of course he wasn't. And neither was I any more. My tattoo was meaningless. I remembered that it would be lasered off, and how much that would hurt, and what a lot of fuss it was over a toe-sized drawing of a fish in a toga. A sizzle broke my reverie. The man scraped a couple of the waffle fish into paper bags and presented them to me.

'*Taiyaki*' is what I think he said.

We thanked him and scraped together whatever Japanese yen were still in our pockets. Then we found a bench, shoved our faces into the bags and inhaled the scent of waffle heaven. Inside the waffles were either a custard paste or something sweet and reddish.

'Japan isn't so bad,' said Alicia, spewing crumbs. Evidently, she'd forgotten about our would-be assassin. And the missing client we'd agreed to protect. And the expulsion from an elite detective agency. Waffles will have that effect on you. The street was flickering to life. There were shopkeepers opening up, a pregnant lady walking a black, brown and white mini-husky, and two schoolchildren waiting by a bus stop.

They caught sight of us and looked as puzzled as the waffle man. They might have been a brother and sister, too – a mirror image of us, in black uniforms and high socks, while we had waffles, a double-bass case and a fart-aholic cat. The badge on their blazers snared my attention. With their stitched lion's paw surrounded by quills, they had to be from Lionpaw Towers. These were Bobo's pupils! Perhaps they would know something! As I stood up, a white coach swept up to the crossroad. The luggage doors whirred open.

'Al,' I said, grabbing her hand. 'We need to get on that bus.'

'Now?'

'Now.'

You might say that an Indiana Jones-style forward roll was excessive, but, believe me, it was the only option. We were swirling into the luggage hold just as the doors slid down. It's interesting what a luggage hold reveals about a school. In here were ski bags, hockey bags, surfboard bags and suitcases with what I'd guess were designer logos on them.

'*Ooooft!*' yowled Alicia as she barged into one of them. 'This school is *swish*!'

'Yep.' I glanced around for something to hide in.

'We doing the whole squeeze-yourself-into-a-suitcase routine again then, Colin?'

'You must be a mind reader.' I saw a cluster of instrument cases. 'Can you fit into your double-bass case?'

'With all the gadgets?' She clicked open the case. 'I guess. Good job I'm not a beanpole like you.' She nestled herself and Bernard in. 'So hopefully they'll just smuggle us into the orchestra pit, tragic horse style?'

'*Trojan* horse, but yep.'

'Leave me a bit of breathing space, yeah?'

I nodded and buckled up her case. The choices weren't so great for me: a violin case or a drum bag. I went for the second option. Sliding out a big bass drum and burying it under a nest of ski bags, I curled myself in. Zipping myself in from the inside with Alicia's hairpin was at least something I had mastered. But still, even after several test runs, the contortion part didn't get any easier. The waffle fish pinballed around our stomachs as the bus heaved up zig-zag bends. Hopefully Lionpaw Towers wasn't far off.

I tried to focus on the case. Firstly, how would we blend in with the other kids in this swish school? Secondly, who would have info? The headteacher? The janitor? The school nurse? Who of those could identify Bobo's enemies? Thirdly, how was the police search going? And were we too late? And fourthly – selfishly – what would life look like without the G.S.L.? Could I still be a detective? Would I still have the energy? That was a deep one. A halt, a playground whistle and a barrage of footsteps announced our arrival.

Being close to the doors, our double-bass and drum cases were carted off first. Whoever was lugging me probably hadn't thought that a bass drum could be so heavy, but they managed to load us onto some kind of cart. This rattled up a ramp, a hard-tiled floor (you become aware of surfaces in a whole new dimension when bundled in pitch darkness) and finally rested in a dark, hopefully private space. A five-minute wait. I listened. I gambled. I emerged from the drum case into a store cupboard. Then I unbuckled Alicia and Bernard, a finger already on my lips to stem any mewling or bawling.

'I got it, I got it,' Alicia whispered. 'You know, a pastille watch with its built-in torch would be *really* helpful now.'

'Don't start.'

'But thankfully I did pilfer me a little flashlight.'

She lit it under her face, Halloween-pumpkin style.

'Just find the door.'

After vaulting an assault course of instrument cases, stage blocks and music stands (those really spike the soft parts), we took it in turns to peer through a keyhole. Our music cupboard was in a corridor, near a changing room or toilet, which was next to a gym hall.

Before I could decide our next course of action, Alicia thrust Bernard into my arms and left the cupboard. Hissing 'come back' was pointless. I heard some crotchety-sounding footsteps, breathed a short prayer and retreated. I had lost my mentor's logbook, but all the same, I didn't think there were enough pages to cover all these misdemeanours. Splitting from your mentor without a plan! I mean, she wasn't even flouting the rules. It was like she had just never grasped the *concept* of rules. Had I taught her nothing? To make matters worse, Bernard mewled, and only stopped when Alicia – thank my lucky stars it was Alicia – scuttled back into the music cupboard. She was holding two sets of school uniform.

'Next time, tell me where you're going, okay?'

'You're welcome.'

'And where did you get those?'

'The kids were in a PE lesson.'

'And what will happen when two schoolkids come back and find their clothes are missing?'

'They'll have their PE kits, I guess.'

'And how is wearing these going to convince anyone we're Japanese schoolkids?'

'Say we're on exchange, like that Russian kid you hung out with in Russia last winter.'

'Exchange students wearing a jumper five

sizes too small for them?'

'Say it's a crop top. You're foreign and weird.
They'll forgive you.'

I lost the will to argue and just squeezed on the
ridiculously small uniform. Alicia's fitted her like a
glove.

'Al,' I asked. 'Are there any purée guns in that
double-bass case?'

She smiled sheepishly and went to the case. 'I
was wondering when you'd ask that.'

Such weaponry was probably not permitted at
Lionpaw Towers, but still, a detective can never be
sure. We tiptoed out, Alicia with the bass case, and
Bernard inside.

It's funny: you travel to the other side of the
world and yet some things never change. In any
school, in any country, the sound of a teacher's
rollicking is always the same. The snippy shoes.
The ear-splitting screech. The pointing. The beads

of spit as they ask who you are, where you're from and what you think you're doing. It's a universal language. As this Japanese teacher/secretary/other screamed at us in the corridor, we both tried the whole 'we're on a foreign exchange' thing. I don't know if she bought it. Then again, what else would two English schoolkids be doing in a Japanese school for the mega-rich?

She clasped a magenta-nailed hand on our shoulders and marched us to the headteacher's office. As we passed along the corridors, with their perfect displays of play-dough volcanos and calligraphy worksheets, we saw, gazing at his reflection in a trophy cabinet, a horribly familiar Putrid Assistant. We were shoved into the headteacher's office, just as he ran a hand through his curls and turned in our direction.

Chapter 20

Our captor left the lion's den. In the centre was the sort of table where war generals push pins around. The headteacher's family photos, propped around the table, softened the war vibe. These displayed their kids in a ballpark, an aquarium, at a prize-giving and at various ages, from freckles to spots to braces to glitter. Crashing us back into reality, two beefcakes in overalls occupied the corner. Janitors? Beefcake One fed leaves into a tank full of stick insects. Beefcake Two flared his nostrils, as if suppressing a sneeze.

At a wall-sized window stood the headteacher, in a beige suit, with her back to us. That classic intimidation tactic. One veiny hand played with a dark gemstone in her ear. I felt something jog. Alicia nudged me and nodded to the windowsill. On it was not something you expect to see in any teacher's possession: a suitcase full – no, *bursting* with money. As if sensing our eyes on the prize, the headteacher turned to us. My camera-brain clicked. A shiver of recognition pinged around my system. The Beige Suit Lady from Octoballs Limited! The fake plastic foods! Bobo's GF! A headteacher at Lionpaw Towers?

'I am told,' she said in a steely monotone, 'that you are exchange students.'

My tongue had apparently turned to lead, so I nodded. I wondered if Alicia was twigging.

'And yet –' she looked at the beefcakes '– I don't recall your faces from the registration process.'

Alicia still had the pep to keep fudging it.

'Must be a system error,' she said sweetly. 'Maybe check it again? We've come a reallllly long way. You've probably never heard of Rufflington-on-Sea, but it's super fa—'

'Cut to the point!' snapped Beige Suit Lady. She was a convincing headteacher. Maybe she *was* a headteacher?

'We've come, er . . .' I racked the brain. And then I thought, why not just be honest? 'We've come about Lord . . . er, *Mr* Bobo.'

Alicia shot me one of her mega-frowns.

'He's our teacher,' she offered. 'And we are reallllly worried about him.'

'Oh, are you?' said Beige Suit. 'That is very kind of you. But that is a matter for the adults of Lionpaw Towers, not the children.'

'But,' I began, 'we'd really like to help. We want to help get him back!'

Beefcake One looked up from his stick insects.

Beefcake Two sneezed. Beige Suit laughed.

'Well, actually, we are arranging this, and we hope to have your teacher, Mr Bobo, back very, very soon.'

'Cool!' said Alicia. 'Is that big bag of cash reward money or something?'

'It's not for you,' said Beige Suit, giving an eye signal to the heavies. 'It's for some very helpful people who are returning poor Mr Bobo back to us.'

'You mean it's ransom money?' shouted Alicia. 'Like, he's been kidnapped and stuff?'

'Al, take it down a peg . . .'

'Very perceptive of you, little . . .' said Beige Suit. 'Er . . . what is your name?'

'People call me Bubble Tea Baby.'

I looked at her. 'Do they?'

Beige Suit picked up the bulging suitcase. 'Thankfully, here at Lionpaw Towers we have a most generous community of prosperous parents, who are only too willing to make a donation to bring back their children's favourite teacher.' She pressed a buzzer. 'Now, I would like you two to register with our reception team . . . Did something just "meow"?'

'We want to come with yooooou!' said Alicia, beaming. 'Let's bring back Bobo together!'

Beige Suit was actually buying this. She liked Alicia and smiled back, her colourful braces sparkling.

'Well, perhaps, if you want to help, you can come and welcome him.'

'Yes!!!!' Alicia went to high-five me. I wasn't in the mood for celebrating. As much as her plan was working to get us to Bobo, wherever he was, there was one small problem. It was hovering in the glass window of the door and its name was Pierce Aniseed.

'Oh, yuck!' said Alicia, scowling back at him.

'Who is that handsome boy?' said Beige Suit.

'Handsome?' said Alicia. 'He's awful. I don't like to be a dobber, you know, but he's been going around stealing younger kids' uniforms!'

The nerve on this girl. I hid behind the double-bass case, hoping it would hide my skimpy, clearly stolen uniform.

'Really?' said Beige Suit. 'That's terrible!'

'Yeah,' continued Alicia, trying not to smile. 'Also, if you're missing a bass drum, that's him, too. I'm not the boss, but I'd put him in detention right away. Before we even leave this office.'

Beige Suit clicked to Beefcake One – maybe they *were* janitors – and instructed him to step out and deal with the Preening Assistant.

'This is crazy!' we heard him shout. 'You can't trust him! You can't trust that sneaky sneak-mouse! He's wanted by the police!' He switched to Japanese, shouting even louder. We could hear him bawling as

Beefcake One led him away. Alicia was on a roll. I needed to warn her not to trust Beige Suit, though. This didn't sit right. Why was she letting us come? Why was she even *here*, in a school for gazillionaires, when surely she had fake cabbages to manufacture?

We followed her and Beefcake Two through the school – so cold and blue, all glass and steel, heads poking up from partitions and kids shuffling to lessons, giggling. Probably at my uniform. Finally, we were outside, with Beige Suit opening the door of a shiny white limousine.

I whispered to Alicia: 'She's Bobo's GF.'

'Clocked it, Col.'

'Just stay on your toes.'

She nodded and made a circle with her thumb and forefinger.

Beige Suit hoisted on a pair of liver-coloured gloves, took the driver's seat and piped in classical music. Beefcake Two sat alongside her, offering zero chat. The limousine snaked around the hilly roads. From the back, we stared at distant islands, lush and hazy. Some resembled bathing dinosaurs, others a snoozing pharaoh's head. A canopy of bubble-wrap clouds rumbled overhead.

Eventually we pulled into a lay-by opposite a dark wooden gate, with carvings of skinny birds and a thatched roof jutting out in several tiers. Beefcake led the way, reaching into his pocket. Hopefully he had more than just rat poison in there, or whatever it is janitors carry, in case these ransomers were tricky. Beige Suit grabbed the suitcase. She definitely wasn't a legit headteacher.

We followed a path into a wooded garden, with mossy stones, shrines and clusters of that famous blossom – the kind on tourist brochures, promising peace and tranquillity. Qualities that don't go hand in hand with being a detective. We saw another postcard image: one of those curved red bridges over a stream with waterlilies. What next? Someone in a patterned kimono with a fan? There was also one of those giant gongs – postcard image number three. And lastly, in the distance, stood a traditional, open-walled building, where some sort of class was taking place. There was a hazardous number of candles, and people on mats following an instructor, soaking up the tranquil vibes. We walked towards the bridge.

As we did, we saw Bobo. He was sitting in a wheelchair, pale and frail. He looked awful. As did his 'carer': The Artist Formerly Known As Rat. Inside my infant's blazer, I felt for the purée gun.

'Bobo!' cried out Beige Suit, and she cantered over the bridge, suitcase in hand. Bobo didn't move a muscle. He looked petrified. TAFKAR smirked. He nudged the wheelchair forward, revealing the source of Bobo's terror: a non-purée gun. I'd never seen a ransom swap before. I didn't think they happened in broad daylight in front of a meditation class (or whatever that was), but what do I know?

TAFKAR wheeled Bobo to Beige Suit, who seemed remarkably calm. She passed the suitcase to TAFKAR. She had her Bobo. TAFKAR had his millions. And that was it. Simple. Except that wasn't it. As TAFKAR walked off, Beige Suit squealed. She and Janitor Beefcake began slapping Bobo's cheek. He wasn't stirring.

'Col . . .' said Alicia. 'Is he, like . . . *dead*?'

Beige Suit now snapped at Beefcake, pointing at TAFKAR. What she said was, at a guess, Japanese for 'GET HIM!!'

Beefcake tore over the bridge. TAFKAR ran towards the building. That meditation class was about to seriously lose its tranquil vibes. Our purée guns came out. Beefcake might have had beefiness, but that was all he had. I was at least expecting *something* of a fight. But TAFKAR simply swung an elbow as sharp as a narwhal's tusk, clonking

Beefcake (maybe he really *was* just a janitor, actually), who then somersaulted over the railing and into the stream.

'Woah!' shouted Alicia.

Beige Suit turned to us. And smiled. I got it. I got it all now. Bobo wasn't dead. He was as realistic looking and perfectly sculpted as a fake plastic cabbage. I ran over to him.

'It's a waxwork!' I shouted.

'Very intelligent, exchange students,' said Beige Suit. She marched over to the heap of Beefcake, who was hauling himself onto the riverbank. All we heard was a *SLAP* and the janitor was out cold. She reached inside his jacket pocket and produced the second very real-looking gun of the day. Unless that was also a waxwork.

'You okay, Al?' I whispered.

'I've been better.'

'Okay, it's really rare that an apprentice actually

has to use their purée gun,' I explained, 'but we sort
of need to.'

'No whispering!' shrieked Beige Suit. She
cackled and began climbing up the bank. Which
was weird, but then it got even weirder. She put
a glove to her hair and wrenched it off! Then
she shook her head and a curly mop of real hair
billowed out. I saw her profile against the tourist-
brochure blossom, and now, finally, I really did see
everything. She climbed onto the bridge.

I somehow croaked it out: '*You're* Mystery Meats!!!!'

Alicia read my mind, as perhaps only sibling
detectives can, and in perfect sync we fired the
molten plum purée.

Chapter 21

I know a poor worker blames their tools, but there is one noticeable flaw with the standard G.S.L.-issue molten purée gun: it's not very accurate. Sure, it'll fire a red-hot, laser-sharp volley of food-fire across several hundred metres, but what good is that when you simply burn a hole in a nearby bridge post? One of us, at least – or perhaps it was a ricochet – caught Mystery Meats in the driving glove. She dropped her own gun and writhed on the floor. Perhaps she'd broken a nail.

We could still see TAFKAR, rounding a bend

in the distance. I didn't feel like chasing him. Then again, I'd feel like a pretty sloppy detective if a suitcase of banknotes went missing on my watch. We shot the last of the purée and this time seemed to catch TAFKAR on the fleshy part of his thigh. He slowed to a hobble. We gained on him as he approached the building that housed the meditation class. He turned and scowled, then looked at the building, assessing his options. The sliding wall revealed a collection of tourists, most of whom were quite elderly, looking very zen.

He began crawling around the side of the building, through the narrow gaps between rocks and plants, looking for somewhere he could lose us. As we crept up the gravel path, I was thankful that the zen brigade had their eyes closed. They were partly screened by the sliding door, which we pressed up against. I could still hear the calming voice of the instructor, getting everyone to go to their happy place.

'Breathe in,' soothed the instructor, 'and breathe out. Nice and slow. Let your body speak to you. Listen to the sounds of your body. Of the breeze. Of the water. Of the –'

'What the *heck* is this?' whispered Alicia. I shrugged. The instructor signalled for the class to take a break, and their murmuring filled the space. Terrible timing. They all stood up and stretched and we couldn't pass the side of the building without being spotted. I peeked my head around and glanced partially into the space. The far wall opened to more garden, with a pond of fat, red-and-white/yellow-and-white fish and a shady bamboo grove.

Calm. Very calm. Except for the sight of TAFKAR staggering around the pond, one hand on the suitcase, the other covering the hole in his trousers. And now more voices filled my ears. Voices that shocked me to my core. It wasn't the voice of Mystery Meats. It wasn't the voice of Pierce Aniseed – who, after all, *wasn't* Mystery Meats. And it wasn't even the voice of Witherknife. No. Worse than that. It started with a grunt.

'Urgggh . . . I'm not as bendy as I used to be, Henrietta!'

No . . . it couldn't be . . . The English woman's voice that replied – 'Henrietta', I'm guessing – confirmed my worst suspicions: 'I'm so glad we've come here, Arnold. It's so calm. So peaceful.'

Arnold!!!!! The familiar snorty voice picked up.

'Did you pack the cream? For my, er, you know . . .'

'This place is just what you needed, Arnold. You gave too much to that school and –'

'Don't mention that hellhole, Henrietta! I'm through with it! I'm – I'm . . .'

'Be calm, Arnold, be calm. Just focus on the koi carp.'

'Yes . . . yes . . . you're quite right, Henrietta . . . calm . . . I'm calm.'

'Remember what the instructor said, Arnold. Listen to your breathing, to the gentle breeze, to the . . . oh my goodness, what's happened to that poor man?'

'What poor man?! Where?! What's happening, Henrietta?'

'That poor man outside with that suitcase . . . he seems to be staggering . . . crawling. Shouldn't we go over and see if he's okay?'

No!!! To my lasting, sweat-festing, toe-curling horror, two English figures waddled into view: Mr (alongside, presumably, Mrs) Hogstein. Here. In Japan. In a meditation class. Standing in the way of me and a deadly criminal.

'This is ridiculous,' muttered Alicia, watching

them plod into the garden in their slippers and dressing gowns. 'As *if* that crank from your big school is here!' They went over to 'check up' on TAFKAR, who was now sprawling towards the grove, dragging the suitcase.

'If you think that's bad,' I said, mopping the monsoon from my forehead, 'turn around.'

'Uh-oh,' said Alicia.

Mystery Meats was striding up the gravel path. On the other side of the class, the Hogsteins were talking to TAFKAR. Talk about being between a rock and a hard place. Then again, I reflected, Hogstein wasn't technically my teacher any more.

'Go, go, go!' I shouted. We charged through the class, skidding over the gym mats, through the open side and across the garden.

'Stoppp!!!!' squealed Mystery Meats, rat-a-tatting after us. TAFKAR 'ahhhed'. Mrs Hogstein 'oooohed'. Hogstein said nothing. His jaw just bungee-jumped, and his glasses misted up with all his snorting. He began to sway, dangerously close to the pond.

'Of all the meditation retreats in the world,' I heard him splutter, 'you had to gate-crash mine.'

'Get out of the way!' I shouted, diving for TAFKAR's suitcase. TAFKAR lashed out. I ducked, but he connected. Something above me made a fleshy sort of *WHUMP* sound. I rolled in a ball through the tangle of limbs, emerging with the suitcase. Mrs Hogstein screamed.

I could almost see the cartoon stars chirruping around my former history teacher's big bald dome after a knuckle sandwich from TAFKAR. I remember seeing his slippers fly off as he ballooned into the air and, almost in slow motion, crashed into the pond, his wife screaming, TAFKAR moaning and Mystery Meats barging through the class.

A suitcase, a bass case, an apprentice, a cat, and we were legging it through the bamboo grove as if our lives depended on it. Which they did. It was so shady, so green, so samey and unfamiliar, we just ran blindly, skidding over rocks and moss, shots and screams ringing through the air. As we approached a clearing, with a bridge and a gorge, we made the fatal error of looking back. I only remember a split second after that: a towering mass of tailcoat, a starchy white towel, a sneering laugh, more cartoon stars and the slats of the bridge crashing into close-up as I finally fell.

Chapter 22

Applause. *That* was what woke me. A TV-studio audience cheering and clapping, piped in from a loudspeaker in a hidden nook of the cave. I guessed it was a cave, squinting at the rough-hewn rockface twisting overhead. A little hand was slapping my cheek, trying to revive me. Gently at first, then harder. Maybe too hard.

'Ouch!'

A wonky blonde fringe and scowling eyes stared into mine.

'You okay, Col?'

'Al . . . where are we?'

'I don't know, but I want to go home.'

'Yep . . .'

'I also want Bernard.'

'They took Bernard?'

She nodded and I almost saw steam puff from her nostrils. The studio audience's applause grew from the surrounding darkness, with a few whoops thrown in. We sat up and, on cue, the harshest, brightest, pinkest spotlights flashed around the cave. A nightmarish scene stretched before us.

'Really?' whispered Alicia.

We were on a podium. Not a good podium, where you receive medals and flowers and praise. More of a rocky podium, surrounded by a sea of stinking fish guts, in what was probably some hot-as-hell oil. There were other podiums ahead, like stepping stones. The stinky sea ran in a long, zig-zagging channel, flanked by archways. At the end of it stood a gold throne. And mounted above it, spot-lit in orange, was the Good Luck Fishcake, in its original glass box. A ladder stretched into shadow.

As we took it in, the audience applause was smothered by a gong. When this finished going off, trumpets tooted a medieval fanfare. A silky voice took over the loudspeaker.

'And now, ladies and gentlemen . . . it's time to play . . . *BATTERED BY THE BUTLER*!!'

With this announcement, a horrible mirage came out from the arches: a dozen tail-coated, wing-collared, white-gloved butlers. Being on brand, they all carried a white cloth. They were also holding a range of instruments for battering purposes. Some had those massive, padded drumsticks; some wielded hockey sticks, while others favoured giant boxing gloves on the end of a pole. I think one guy even had a mace. Among them, of course, was Witherknife. He held a microphone. The head butler. The head batterer. That was no surprise. What happened next, though, was.

'And now . . .' purred Witherknife into the microphone, 'please welcome your host: the one, the only, the iconic, the inimitable, Lord Boboooooooooooo!!!!!'

The trumpets re-tooted. The applause whooped up a gear. The lights flashed from pink to yellow to acid green. Sliding down the ladder, clad in neon-pink-and-green tweed, sparkly bowler hat and kaleidoscopic waistcoat and tie, an umbrella over his arm, was the man we had come here to rescue. Lord Bobo. He landed and waved to an imaginary audience like the saddo he was. Then he plonked himself on the throne, crossed his big flamingo legs and raised a monocle to his eye. He saw our startled-deer faces and laughed.

'Ah . . . welcome, Detective Anchovy . . . and, er, your apprentice, whose name I'm not familiar with.'

'People call me Grubbin' Hood.'

'I see. I'm sure, children, you are wondering what this is all about.' He held up a hand as Alicia went to chip in, cutting her off. 'I'm sure, children, you are desirous for a window into the workings of an utter genius.'

'Come to the wrong place then,' Alicia whispered.

'Silence!!!! No talking!!' Lord Bobo clicked his fingers and two more figures emerged from the arches: Mystery Meats and TAFKAR. TAFKAR assembled a tripod and camera, pointing it at the stepping stones.

'I have brought you here,' continued Bobo, 'to play a little game. I call it –'

'Battered by the Butler?' I ventured.

'Do not interrupt me, child. Yes, I call it Buttered by the Battler – I mean, Battled by the Butter – I mean . . . stop giggling, child!'

I nudged Alicia.

'Anyway,' Bobo went on, 'through my genius, I have recreated the iconic gameshow of the 1990s, of which I was the STAR, which I shall re-record and pitch to the studio execs, and, with the blessings of the Good Luck Fishcake, become a TV gazillionaire once more!!!!!'

'By "through your genius",' I said, 'you mean through the stolen ransom money of mega-rich parents from Lionpaw Towers, which you shamelessly conned them out of.'

Alicia nodded, giving him a super-scowl.

'You played the victim . . . and all along . . .' I petered out, deflated.

'How very clever of you, little boy,' chuckled Bobo. 'It *is* a shame that you've been fired from that ridiculous little detective agency, isn't it?'

Mystery Meats, TAFKAR and Witherknife smirked, loyal cronies that they were.

'This must be very disappointing for you, Detective Anchovy,' Bobo continued. 'But I will give you one last chance. I am a sportsman, after all.' He reached around the throne and produced the suitcase of all the parents' megabucks. Or mega-yen, I should say.

'If,' said Bobo, 'you can get from where you are to here, and get this suitcase off me, I will, of course, release you. In order to do that, though, you must play . . .'

The twelve butlers now raised their instruments and boomed: 'BATTERED BY THE BUTLER!!!!'

'Simply dodge the battering of these twelve sterling fellows,' said Bobo, 'and avoid the pool below you, and you will have my mercy. In fact . . .' He stroked his chin. 'Let me make this a little fairer for you. Witherknife, *come here!!*'

It was strange to see Witherknife, this ten-foot human panther, sidle up to Bobo like a terrified kitten, but he did. Bobo stood and advanced towards him.

'You have disappointed me, Witherknife.'

'Have I, my lord?' purred Witherknife, first speaking into the microphone, in the role, then dropping it, realising that all was not well.

'Indeed you have, Witherknife. You've put the entire operation at risk. You failed to stop this little brat detective and his little brat apprentice on several occasions. Therefore, you have disappointed me. You have *failed me.*'

And backing Witherknife to the edge of the stink-pool, he poked him with his umbrella. When you're as heavy as that butler was, gravity does the rest. Witherknife tumbled.

'My Lorrrrrrrrrrrrrrrd Boboooooo, nooooooo!!!!' he moaned, disappearing into the hot, fishy oil with a nasty sizzle. The eleven other butlers gave a sharp gasp. Bobo spun around.

'TAFKAR!' he shouted. 'Come here!'

TAFKAR, not the brightest artist in the drawer, shuffled up.

'My Lord Bobo. In Japan, we have an expression. We say that when the rat has brought home cheese, the other animals —'

'For goodness' sake shut up, TAFKAR! You, too, have failed me.'

'No, Lord Bobo. No, Lord Bobo! Please, Lord Bobo!'

The umbrella shoved. TAFKAR tumbled. Again the fish pit, again the horrid sizzle. Mystery Meats, the brightest of the cronies — and, you have to hand it to her, a terrific actor — darted off into the shadows.

'Oh well,' laughed Bobo. 'That ought to show them! I am *not* –' he glared at us '– I repeat, I am *not* horsing around. You *will* play Battered by the Butler, and you *will* do as I say. Butlers?'

The eleven jittery butlers readied themselves. 'Begin battering!!'

Chapter 23

As with Hogstein crashing into the pond, there was a slow-motion quality to the way Lord Bobo collapsed. It's often that way when someone falls. You can't really believe it's happening, so your brain shows the images with a pixellated lag. I just saw the halo of light above the ladder, and the black form plunge down as a bat-like blur. So it was only when it crashed onto Bobo that I realised what it was: Alicia's double-bass case.

Even more bizarrely, it had been lobbed down by a <u>P</u>ernickety <u>A</u>ssistant.

'Aniseed!' I shouted. He just had time to slide down the ladder and fling us the case before a butler walloped him. When it matters, you catch things. Even if those things are whopping great double-bass cases hurtling through the air.

We clicked it open and used it as a shield, grabbing a few objects from inside. These were a) the bubble-tea bazooka, and b) the turbo-charged pogo stick. The butlers gave us their worst. But Alicia bubble-tea-bazooka-ed with all the fury of a girl who's been robbed of her favourite cat.

I found a spare purée gun and fired. Two butlers got a taste of their own battering medicine and plunged into the oil. Aniseed put the hours sculpting his six-pack into use, knocking off two, no, three butlers. But there were still way more. And Bobo was getting away – shimmying up the ladder with the suitcase of money. The coward.

'Alicia!' I shouted, squatting down. 'Jump on my shoulders.'

'But I'm not done bazoo—'

'I don't care!! Get on!!'

She sighed and climbed on. I hit the green button on the turbo-charged pogo stick. It was the first time I'd used it. I had no idea if it actually worked. And it wouldn't have been the best time to find out if it didn't. We gave it a mini-spring and then, as if blasted from a cannon, we rocketed up, out of reach of the battering butlers. Then down again, praying we'd connect with another podium. We did. And we rocketed up again, plunging down onto another.

Bobo was scuttling up the ladder like a neon-pink tarantula. Our third jump had us almost level. We leapt forward, arms flailing, groping for the ladder. Our luck held out. Below, Aniseed was outnumbered, despite taking out another three batterers. We couldn't just *leave* him there . . .

Scurrying down, Alicia grabbed his hand and we ushered him onto the ladder as I took aim at the remaining butlers. One got molten-puréed in the toe, *ouch*. One gave up and vanished into the arches – sensible. The other staggered after us, a few rungs below.

Aniseed was huffing, struggling, but he still had the strength to shove his size-ten boot down onto the butler, who clattered onto Bobo's throne. Ahead, the last shred of pink-and-green trouser leg vanished out of the opening of the cave. Seconds later we surfaced, too, gasping in the air. We crawled out into another bamboo grove. The air was thick with the tang of rain and the distant, rumbling sea. Bobo, as badly camouflaged as he could possibly be, was darting up the hill.

Aniseed was limping.

'Guys,' he sighed. 'I'm sorry. I can't . . . I can't . . .' He slumped against a fallen log. 'Aargh!

This stupid ingrown toenail always screws me up!'

'Chillax, Pierce,' said Alicia. 'I'm sure there are more gentle sports you can play.'

For the first time since we'd met him, he gave a genuine laugh. 'You two are okay . . . I'm sorry, I guess I was a bit of a whoosh-bag before . . .'

'A *bit*?' said Alicia.

'Yeah, but he did sort of save our lives, Al, so we can call it quits, right?'

'Okaaaay.'

'Right,' I said, staring at the neon-pink speck slipping through the trees. 'You two stay here.'

'I'll alert the coastguards . . .' said Pierce, groggily typing into his G.S.L. watch. 'But hurry!'

I headed up the grove, squinting through the rain. The purée gun was out of juice. I had no idea how to stop a demented English-lord stereotype who was unafraid to wield an umbrella. Glimpses of the sea flickered through the trees. Bobo darted on, and up. The path zig-zagged until the trees thinned, and a riot of colour pulsed beyond them: the pink-and-yellow Battenberg-cake stripes of a hot-air balloon, waiting on the clifftop.

The rain intensified until it was basically a wall of solid water, churning up the hill into a mudslide. Bobo's orange-and-purple spats would've been perfect on some loopy catwalk for an English gent's collection. But they weren't as good for running in this swamp as my scruffy trainers. Something about the mud encouraged me to just go for it. As the ground levelled, I dived at his legs.

I felt the CRACK of his knobbly knees connecting with my nose. The old gent's spats connecting with my sternum. And though that hurt, Bobo tumbled. The suitcase was airborne. He sprang back up, and another spat connected with my chin. I somersaulted backwards.

'Curse you, Mark Anchovy!!!' he roared, his

moustache askew, his bowler dented, his monocle shattered. He raised his umbrella and I crawled backwards, perilously close to the cliff edge.

'CURSE YOU, MARK ANCHOVY! I WILL END YOU! I WILL DESTR–'

He had shimmied to the right but was too angry to notice the white fluffy thing behind him. It was the softest of knocks, but sometimes the softest will do. He was too startled to cry out. I had screwed up my eyes, preparing for the clobbering – so that was the last I ever saw of Lord Bobo. Bernard mewled at me, his green eyes glowing. I rolled on my side and peered over the cliff. The suitcase had landed in a tree. Judging by the blazer and bowler hat bobbing on the sea, Bobo hadn't been so lucky.

Bernard snuggled up to me. It was almost as comforting as the siren, and the red-and-blue light scattering over the waves, as the police speedboats cut across the bay.

Chapter 24

As if in fear, a fried egg quivered on Princess Skewer's fork. She gazed out of the fogged-up window of Fryer Tuck's diner at the wet jumble of London. We waited for her answer as she mopped up her fry-up. I rattled the metal lid on my teapot, which just irked her even more. Or maybe it was the sight of Bernard trying to sniff the toast rack. Alicia yanked him back.

'It's going to be a fluffing head-fluff,' said Princess, 'to explain to Isadora Bobo that her dad, whom she's paid us a truckload of moula to find, is in fact a thieving, power-crazed nut job.'

She dabbed a blob of ketchup from the corner of her mouth.

'But, then again, that's why I'm paid to be the boss and you're not.'

It was a hard pill to swallow. Lord Bobo led us up the garden path. (Or is it down the garden path?) We'd schlepped across the globe and almost been killed trying to protect this guy, and all along he'd been getting his waxwork cast, his getaway hot-air balloon ready and his millions secreted. He couldn't hack not being famous. And being a seasoned crackpot, he tried to reverse all that by ransoming himself in order to con money from billionaire parents, staging a lunatic gameshow and hedging his bets on a stolen Good Luck Fishcake. (Which was now reinstalled at the restaurant – hopefully with some lasers guarding it.) I felt sick thinking about the whole thing. But

I couldn't imagine how Isadora must be feeling. A supervillain father. Ouch.

Pierce Aniseed strutted over to our table to clear away the plates. He still wasn't mega-chummy, but at least he didn't look at us like something he'd trodden in.

'What happens now?' I said.

'Are we still expelled?' said Alicia.

Princess drained her coffee and smiled.

'Well . . . it *is* a lot of paperwork to get you re-admitted and you did cause us a mahoosive amount of hassle, but . . .'

Alicia widened her eyes.

'But?'

' . . . But . . . you *did* also show great enterprise in tackling Lord Bobo and uncovering his sick, sad plan.'

'So that's a yes?'

Princess looked at Pierce. 'I get that you three

may have had your beef, but we can put that aside now, right, Pierce?'

It was still a struggle for him. But he nodded, sighed, gave the best morsel of a smile we could've hoped for and carried off the grease-spattered plates.

'Oh, I almost forgot,' said Princess, passing us a light-blue envelope. 'This arrived for you from the Tokyo branch, courtesy of Skeleton Key.'

The envelope contained a formal letter from Skeleton Key, a nice note from Monmon (probably in her non-writing hand) and two pin badges.

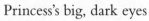 These contained the pink spiral within the *hanamaru* symbol that Japanese children get for extra-special homework, which in turn was flanked by golden spatulas. Princess's big, dark eyes

went even bigger when she examined the badges.

'*Taihen yoku dekimashita*,' she said.

'What's that?' I asked. (I didn't get through *all* my Japanese phrase book.)

'It means very, very well done,' said Princess. 'Those are Japanese G.S.L. medals for special acts of bravery.'

'Bernard helped, too, you know,' said Alicia.

'I can't believe you've smuggled in that mangy alley cat,' sighed Princess, still disgusted by the sight of him.

'Alley cat!' said Alicia. 'Col – I mean, er . . . Anchovy . . . how about if my codename is Allie Alley Cat?'

Princess rolled her eyes.

'Yeah . . .' I said and ruffled her hair. 'That kind of works, Al. From now on, when we're working, I'll call you Allie Alley Cat.'

'Yessssssssss!'

'Pierce!' called Princess. 'The tattoo pen, please.'

Aniseed re-emerged with a small silver box, which I remembered from when I'd completed my first assignment.

'Really, Anchovy,' Princess said, 'you should've given your apprentice – sorry, Allie Alley Cat – at least a provisional tattoo . . . Where is this going then?'

'I want one like my brother's,' said Alicia.

'If you insist,' said Princess. 'Place your foot on the table.'

If she wasn't Branch President of an elite detective agency, I have to say, Princess could've made a killing as a tattooist. Fingers of steel. She didn't even need a magnifying glass to draw, in

 minute detail, a winking cat's face on Alicia's third toe, below the diamond of spatulas. Despite a very ticklish apprentice.

We polished off a sticky toffee pudding as
we waited for the ink to dry, then Princess led
us through the diner to the storeroom, where
we saw a dark, puffy nest of hair bending over
a switchboard. The nest looked up and we saw
Camillo, who put down his soldering iron and gave
us both a hug.

'I am so glad to see you back!' he said.

'You deserve a proper break, you two,' said
Princess. 'Cam, we need to get these detectives
home. Shuttle them to the Rufflington train
station, please.'

Camillo nodded and opened the sliding door of
the deep-chest freezer. 'You need to climb inside,
please.'

'Into that?'

'Trust him, Allie Alley Cat – it's totally fine.'

'Cold, no?'

'Do not worry,' said Camillo. 'This is only a

fake freezer. It is actually comfortable and quite nice to travel in.'

She climbed in. We somehow wedged her double-bass case *and* Bernard in as well. Camillo pulled a hatch from the wall, which looked like a box of marshmallow twists but was actually a control panel, pushed some buttons and slid Alicia's 'carriage' forward so I could climb into the following one.

'Good job, Anchovy,' said Princess. 'Eventually.'

'Thanks,' I sighed. 'It's a tough gig, this mentoring business.'

'Welcome to my world.'

She winked and slipped out of sight. Camillo smiled down on me as I lay on the fake frozen peas and saluted.

'*Arrivederci*, Anchovy.'

The door shuttered over me, the carriage rumbled and we were off, gliding through the underbelly of London and then out into the sticks, to the coast, to sleepy Rufflington-on-Sea. Our half-term 'holiday' was over, and our parents would be at the station.

It was always odd to switch back to Colin Kingsley mode after a hair-raising mission as Mark Anchovy. But I was glad to get back to normality. There'd be a big whack of cash winging its way to Caesar Pizza – our parents still thought it was an insane tipper – and the secret office would stay, and Alicia had become a detective after all. But I was tired. Really tired. And sometimes I wondered if being a detective was all it was cracked up to be. At least there would be no Hogstein when we went back to school. There would be Dexter, though. Oh well.

I was trying to work out if there was any homework for the first day back when a bright light flooded the carriage. The mocking squawk of seagulls told me we were home. The faces of

Yelena and Yaconda swung in and helped me out.

'*Konichiwa!*' said Yelena in a baby voice.

'*O-genki desu ka?*' said Yaconda, in a grandaddy voice.

'I'm too tired for Japanese,' I burbled.

We had surfaced in the coffee shop in Rufflington train station. Thankfully the hair-gelled guy who normally worked there was on his day off. Alicia had already disembarked and was kicking her legs on a chair in the corner. Bernard was swiping at the cord of an apron.

'Oh,' said Yaconda, in a strict-governess voice, 'they'll need this – don't forget, Lena.'

'I didn't forget, Yack, you distracted me!' said Yelena, in a grunty, snorty voice. She went to the store cupboard and brought out Alicia's double bass, which had somehow been recovered from the National Children's Jazz Orchestra's band camp at the country mansion.

'Come on, Al,' I said. 'Open up your case and put this in.'

'But . . .' said Alicia.

'What?'

She opened up the case and the bubble-tea bazooka, the turbo-charged pogo stick and a few other bits and pieces tumbled out.

'Alic– Alley Cat: you can't take those *and* the double bass home.'

'But . . .'

'There'll always be next time,' said Yaconda, in a reassuring sales-pitch voice.

'Yeah, we'll keep them safe for you,' said Yelena, in a salty sea-captain voice. 'Oh . . . Anchovy, weren't you supposed to have been in Cornwall with that kid in your class who is, like, *always* sleeping?'

'Please don't mention sleep to me now. Robin, yep.'

'Here,' said Yaconda. 'I thought this might help convince your parents.'

She handed me a little plastic bag that said 'Cornish Souvenirs' on it, with a duffed-up box of clotted-cream fudge inside.

'And I had the even *better* idea of giving you some socks full of sand for authenticity, but Yack wouldn't hear of it,' said Yelena, in what I think was her normal voice.

'Thanks, you two,' I said, taking the double-bass case, as Alicia gathered Bernard. 'I really appreciate your help.'

'See you around, Kingsleys.'

Speaking of Kingsleys, we were only just out of the café and into the waiting room when the spluttering, tank-like clank of a 1980s Volvo filled the car park.

'Cooo-eeeeeee!' wailed my mum so everyone in the town plus the next one over could hear.

'Whose cat is that?' asked my dad, in his deep, searching monotone.

'Mine now,' said Alicia, pressing Bernard tightly to her chest. 'Pleeeeeeeeeeease?'

'Let's decide this at home,' said my mum, piling us all into the car. 'Oooh, clotted-cream fudge!'

The streets of Rufflington, with their mobility carts and punning shop signs and timeworn red postboxes, raced by in a jet-lagged haze. Caesar Pizza, and the statue of Markus Anchovius, flickered into view. We trundled up to the flat and flopped onto our beds. The bathwater gurgled next door over the murmur of our parents debating if Bernard could stay. As the fishy waft of a Mark Anchovy pizza meandered up through the floorboards, we were summoned downstairs.

'Pizza?' asked my mum, slinging it onto the counter.

'Erm . . .' I said, my stomach still sagging with Fryer Tuck's stodge.

'I think I'm still on Japan time,' said Alicia, like the rookie she was.

'Japan time?' asked my dad.

'I mean . . .' she scrambled, looking around the kitchen. 'Japan time? I said . . . the PAN . . . *fried*. THE PAN FRIED.'

'Right . . .' said my dad.

'I'll have a slice, please,' I said, trying to change the subject from an illicit trip to the other side of the planet.

'Sure,' said my mum, giving me three slices.

Alicia winked and made a circle out of her finger and thumb.

'Smooth,' I muttered, and reached for the pizza.